ELLIE QUIN BENEATH THE NEON SKY
(Book 3 of the Ellie Quin Series)

BY

Alex Scarrow

OMNIPEDIA:
[Human Universe: digital encyclopedia]

Article: 'The Legend of Ellie Quin' > Genetic Science

Many a student of history today, at some point, wonders why people in the 20th and 21st centuries were so obsessed with *robots*. One can't help but find amusing those clips from the beginning of the new millennium, of presenters and technology pundits telling their viewing audience that one day in the near future every household would be waited on hand-and-foot by some silicon servant. In fact, there is a very famous antique news clip from 2002 of a bipedal, man-sized robot, walking slowly and falteringly up a set of stairs. The robot was called 'Asimo' and it was built by a company called 'Honda'. This unremarkable achievement was met by rapturous applause and the flashing of camera lights, and represented back then the very height of robotic technology.... the ability to walk up a set of stairs.

With hindsight we know that, when this moment was recorded for posterity, the science of robotics and artificial intelligence, 'cybernetics' as they dubbed it, was on the verge of being sidelined by a technology that would wholly eclipse it. From our vantage point here in the present, it is too easy to look back over time and be amused at their primitive attempts to build living, thinking, moving beings from metal and silicon.

Genetic science pushed all of that to one side.

Throughout the fifteen hundred years from the birth of genetic science to the time of Ellie Quin, this science grew to become the nuts and bolts of society itself. Genetics provided most of the technology-crutches that cybernetics had at one time promised. For example, instead of robots building the world of the future, genetic technology gave us GEN-IMPs (**GEN**etic **I**ndustry and **M**anufacturing **P**ersonnel), known colloquially at the time as 'jimps'. These were engineered bipedal, four-armed, drone workers with simple brains and life spans that could be adjusted to suit the job. This laboratory-made species was responsible for most of the hard physical labor across Human Space, and at the peak of their use these squat, pale skinned creatures were a common enough sight in every construction project on every planet in Human Space.

Genetic science back then was used in almost every facet of life: food production, pharmaceuticals, computers, textiles, plastics.

The human population itself became a genetic product.

Fertility amongst woman had declined to the point where natural childbirth no longer occurred. New generations were instead engineered. This provided the opportunity for the authorities to *enhance* the babies they produced for eager parents, supposedly to better cope with the varied hardships of the new colonial worlds being tamed.

Actually, they were being carefully manipulated by the Administration to be more pliable, docile, compliant….to be obedient little consumers content to leave complicated and important matters, like running the universe, to those in power. Some of the less charitable of historians today wonder whether the IQ of the general population of Ellie's time differed that much from the gene-imps that worked amongst them.

User Comment > Anonymous
We wuz all once ugly mutants. I saw pictures of the freaks from Ellie Quin's time.

Why did they make people so ugliez back then?

User Comment > GenePool
Want to be bigger, gentlymen? Want to be longer, wider for the ladeez? Get insta-gene implants to make your Mr Happy, happy.

User Comment > LostAndLonely
I don't need a man with a big schlong. I need a man with a big heart. Is there an insta-gene implant for that? Doubt it.

User Comment > KozzlePudz
You Humanz obsessed with reproductions. How you creatures evolve into space beat me.

CHAPTER 1

'Hufty, it's me again. Well now, what can I say? It's been an incredibly busy few weeks. There's so much to tell you that it's hard to know where exactly to start. Okay, let me start this way....' Ellie paused for a moment and passed the voice-diary from one hand to the other.

'So, I had this whacko idea about a month ago. The idea was...running shuttle visits up to the north polar region. You see, Aaron had lost his regular shuttle contract, and Jez and I were struggling to find any decent work in the city. It just seemed to fit everyone's needs. So, stupidly, I thought getting Jez and Aaron together and blurting the idea out in front of them might be a smart thing to do. I couldn't have been more wrong,' said Ellie wearily as she sat down for a moment on the crate beside her. Her arms ached painfully from the work she had done so far this morning.

'They liked the idea so-o-o much...I'm here right now inside Aaron's shuttle painting the inside of this daggy cargo hold.'

Ellie surveyed her progress. This was her sixth day on the job, sloshing white paint on to the pitted metal walls with a brush on an extended pole to reach the very top, where the walls curved and became the roof of the cargo hold. She was beginning to wonder whether there was ever going to be an end to this interminable task. She had spent the previous week scrubbing the very same metal walls with detergent to remove several decades' worth of encrusted grime. Every exposed inch of her skin was either smeared with grease, smudged with grime, or dotted with white flecks of paint, or all three.

'I definitely pulled the cruddiest job. Jez's gone into New Haven, sorting some things out, and Aaron has just left to talk to some ship-fitters. So it's just me here on black-pad 79 with the shuttle. Just me and, of course, *Harvey*.'

Ellie shot a quick glance across the hold towards the jimp working silently and diligently with another brush on the opposite wall. 'Aaron bought a jimp at an auction. It was from some construction company that was shutting down, or gone out of business or something. Harvey's only got another three or four months left on his license, then we'll need to re-register him.'

She watched the creature work methodically, carefully dipping the brush into the tub of paint beside it.

For some reason she thought of Harvey as a *him*. Silly really seeing as the thing had no sex organs. However, both Jez and Aaron both referred to him as *IT*, and despite Ellie's insistence, rarely referred to him as *Harvey*, her choice of name of course. It seemed to suit him.

'Harvey's a great little worker,' she said smiling fondly at the jimp. 'And he's a clever little thing too. He understands a lot more, I think, than people give him credit for. Aaron's put me in charge of him, said I was bossy enough that I might as well have my own *staff* to help me with tidying up this cruddy hold.'

Harvey stopped for a moment, recognizing that his recently given name had been spoken aloud. He turned to look at Ellie, the pale grey skin above his beady black eyes furrowed into a worried-looking frown.

'Hey, it's okay Harvey,' she called out, 'I'm just recording my diary. It's okay, you go back to work, there's a good boy,' she reassured him in a soft voice.

The jimp nodded once dutifully, turned back around and resumed carefully applying whitewash to the wall, all four muscular arms working the extended brush rhythmically up and down.

'They say these gene-imps are engineered not to have any feelings at all, and that they have a maximum intelligence that's roughly, like, the same as a six or seven year old child. I think. I'm not so sure though. I reckon Harvey's smarter than that, and I'm pretty sure he feels some sorts of emotions too. I've never seen his mouth smile or anything like that, but his eyes sometimes seem to look happy or sad. I don't know, I guess it's hard to tell for certain if he's feeling or thinking anything.'

She pulled herself up onto her feet, feeling the aching fatigue ripple up her legs, back, and upper arms, and crossed the floor towards him, her boots clunking noisily against the metal grill floor and echoing around Lisa's empty cargo hold.

'Harvey?'

The jimp carefully placed the brush down and turned round slowly to look at her.

Ellie spoke slowly and clearly. 'I am going to get some water to drink. Would you like to have some?'

'Yaasss, Missss Eh-leeee,' he replied quietly, the sibilants exaggerated by his long narrow tongue.

'You take a rest for a few minutes, okay?'

His eyebrows furrowed once more. She knew that the gesture meant a momentary confusion, but actually it made him look worried, like the weight of the world was temporarily resting on his muscular shoulders. Ellie made a sleeping gesture, closing her eyes and placing a palm against one cheek. 'Rest….take a break? Yeah?'

Harvey finally nodded, the worried frown gradually faded from his face as he worked out what she was saying to him.

'Ressssting,' he said gently and settled down onto the floor on his haunches, wrapping his arms around his knees.

'I will be back in a few minutes,' said Ellie as she headed towards the back of the hold and down the ramp onto the landing pad.

The long-stay pad was 'recessed' right now. It had been lowered down from the large plasticrete landing field above into this isolated and air-filled maintenance hangar. Ellie preferred it when the pad had been up. From the cramped comfort of the shuttle's cockpit she had been able to happily watch the comings and goings of craft all day and all night long; the streams of surface-to-orbit barges descending from the sky, the regular arrivals of surface shuttles down into the giant caldera in which New Haven nestled. However, with work being done on Lisa inside and out, the ship needed to be down in the air-filled hangar. She felt cut off from the busy world outside, and a little claustrophobic, despite its immense size.

She walked around the outside of the shuttle, her footsteps echoing off the dark walls of the hangar, and noted with a weary sigh how much more work Lisa needed to have done on the outside before she was presentable enough to be considered a *recreational vessel*. The hull was a drab brown, the last fading scabs of paint from a previous lifetime were all but gone, blasted and scoured by the winds and sands of the planet. It had been Jez's suggestion to also paint the outside white, like snow....giving the shuttle the look as if it had been designed from the very beginning to be an arctic vehicle.

Yeah, thanks a yahoo for that *suggestion, Jez.*

She went back inside the shuttle, walking up a smaller entry ramp at the front beneath its snub nose, and entered the front cabin; Aaron's scruffy home.

Inside she picked her way through the chaotic mess of the cabin towards the galley, placed a plastic jug beneath the water faucet and hit the button.

'So, Hufty, I'm cleaning up and decorating the cargo hold right now,' she said, resuming her diary entry. 'It's really totally scraggy, shitty work, but you know what? I don't think I mind. It's kinda cool.'

Despite moaning about it, despite the aching fatigue in her arms and back. It felt good. It felt like this might just be her first proper step forward. The first glimmer of hope that she might one day follow in Sean footsteps and find a way off Harpers Reach.

'Aaron says that one day, if he earns enough money, he's going to buy a small interplanetary shuttle. One of those medium sized freighters that can lug goods from one planet to another within a solar system. Crud, that would be totally-hoobie doing that, to see a world from orbit, to actually be IN space, it gives me chills just thinking about it!'

She hit the button again to turn the faucet off, picked up the plastic jug and two tumblers, and headed out of the cabin and down the ramp back onto the hangar floor.

'But that's probably a way off yet, Aaron says. It's all going to depend on whether we can make a go of this polar-run thing. Jez's convinced there're enough *toppers* in the city…stupid rich people, the ones who live in the upper-most floors, the penthouses, to make us rich too.'

She rounded the back of the shuttle and proceeded up the loading ramp into the cargo hold once more.

'I did some maths Hufty, just to work it out, just to work out how long it would take to buy a ticket off-world, and out of the system. So…it costs about thirty thousand creds to buy a jump-ticket to another system aboard one of the cheaper freight ships. If we can really make the money Jez thinks we can, that's about a hundred polar-runs….say three or four years, doing it, say, three times a month. That's if we save every cred though,' she said then paused to think about how long four years actually was.

Three or four years? She'd be twenty-three, twenty-four years old by the time she left Harpers Reach. A good age to be exploring the universe she decided.

She knelt down beside Harvey, who rocked gently on his flat feet.

'Well, that's me done for now Hufty. There's a crap-load of work to do.'

She snapped off the voice-diary, poured a glass of water into one of the tumblers and held it out to Harvey.

The jimp uncertainly held a calloused hand out towards the offered cup.

'Yeah, that's right…that's yours, Harvey.'

'Water, Misss Eh-leeeee?'

'Yes, water.'

He gently slid his fingers around the cup and took it from her, pouring it carefully into his small lipless slash of a mouth.

'There's a good boy,' she said.

Harvey drained the plastic tumbler and passed it back to her.

CHAPTER 2

Ellie and Jez packed up and quit their cube just before the end of the four week rent-cycle, still owing a month's rent. But, hey. Jez knew if they stayed another night they would be paid a visit by the tower's security guards and tossed unceremoniously out into the street.

Ellie was surprised at how much *stuff* they had accumulated between them in such a small living space. Most of it of course was Jez's; clothes and shoes mainly. She was glad they had brought Harvey along to help with the carrying.

'I don't think Aaron's going to be pleased if we turn up with all of this you know Jez.'

Jez was in a testy mood. 'I'm not going to throw all this stuff away. This is quality clobber, girl.'

Ellie shrugged. There was that tone of finality in her voice. It was up to Jez then. There was no way Aaron was going to let her fill up his cockpit with her stuff; she would just leave it to the pair of them to debate the matter later on.

'And what about the toob, Ellie?'

Ellie looked at it with a hint of distaste. Frankly she could live without it. The endless sopas, and bleating commercials promising her everything and anything if she'd only buy this, that or the other, had begun to irritate her. Back on the farm, the toob had been her only real window on the world. Living aboard the shuttle, the cockpit's large scuffed, plexitex windscreen would make a much better one.

'Let's leave it. It's only a cheap one anyway.'

Jez's eyes widened with horror.' Leave it!? I'm sorry Ellie-girl, I need my fix! You can't expect me to miss Shuttlestop 7, and Sons and Daughters, can you?'

'I suppose we'll need to put one in the cargo hold with the passengers,' Ellie mused aloud.

'Exactly! They'd expect at least *one* toob aboard.'

They quit the cube late in the evening, both girls and the jimp laden with plastic bags crammed to bursting point with clothing and bedding. Harvey carried the toob projector under one arm, the much heavier FoodSmart in another two, and his fourth strung through the handles of half a dozen more bags.

As Ellie prepared to close and lock the oval door on their cube for the last time, Jez cast one final, doe-eyed glance back inside. 'I've lived in that cube for the last five years of my life,' she said with a wan smile on her lips. 'I've had six cube-chiks live there with me - you were the sixth, Ellie. And you were the one to finally get me off my butt and move out of it.'

Ellie smiled. 'Job done, then.'

Jez laughed away any thought of tears. It was, after all, just a cruddy little habi-cube in one of the more squalid towers in town.

'Thank you for rescuing me Jez.'

'Bah, don't get gloopy on me. I only took you in because I needed someone to clean up after me.'

They rode the skyhound in relative discomfort. There were few people travelling across the city at that time of night. Ellie noticed one or two glances towards Harvey from the scant passengers aboard. Although jimps were a common enough sight on construction projects, they were expensive enough that only the top-dwellers in New Haven could afford them one as a *domestic*. Ellie supposed it looked odd that the pair of them should appear to have money enough to own their own jimp, but not enough to travel privately in their own air car.

Harvey looked nervously out of the window as the busy, twinkling city passed by below them. His eyebrows were furrowed deeply with a look of concern and she noticed his slitted mouth quivered slightly.

Nervous flyer. That was definitely an expression of anxiety on his little face.

It was an often stated claim made by all gene-imp producers universe-wide that these creatures were genetically designed to lack the capacity to feel *any* emotion whatsoever. It was that specific assertion that ensured no-one need feel guilty about how they treated these poor things. Looking at the subtle ticks and movements on Harvey's face right now, Ellie wasn't entirely convinced they understood their genetic products.

'It's okay Harvey, we're perfectly safe.'

Jez sighed and shook her head. 'Ellie, you're such a butterhead.'

'He's scared.'

'He's a machine….that's all. He's a meat power tool, that's it. Aaaggghh - look, you've got me calling it *him* now.'

Ellie smiled, she nudged Harvey gently. 'See, you're slowly winning her round.'

They arrived at the port exit in the Industrial Sector as it approached midnight. The usually crowded immigration hall was deserted and passing through, flashing their ID cards and their landing-pad passes, they arrived via the service tunnel at their submerged black pad hanger half an hour later.

Aaron was sound asleep in his bunk as they tiptoed inside the cabin and both squeezed awkwardly into the lower bunk together, Harvey curling up on the floor beside it.

*

The next morning, over breakfast, they sat on the floor of the cargo hold, which was now, encouragingly, looking a lot less like the inside of a large rusting skip.

'The fitters are coming in today to put in the viewing ports,' announced Aaron as he slurped a scalding mouthful of stewed coffee. He pointed to each of the long walls of the cargo hold. 'There and there, they'll cut out a panel about eight feet long and four feet high, and then install reinforced, double-paneled, plexitex viewing blisters.'

'Oh good,' said Ellie, 'because it feels like a psycho-cube right now.'

'It actually looks a lot better than I thought it would, now you've painted it, Ellie,' said Jez, looking around.

'Yeah,' nodded Aaron. 'Although you missed a bit over there,' he said pointing towards the roof.

Ellie sighed an oh-ha-ha sigh.

'Tomorrow, I've got some ship-fitters coming in to install a toilet pod and then, they're also running a power feed through from the front cabin to here somewhere so we can power the FoodSmart and heating, O2 system and other bits and pieces. Any ideas where we would want to put those things?'

'I've been thinking about that.' Jez got up and walked across the hold towards one of the long walls. 'One of the viewing windows here, right?'

Aaron nodded.

'I think if we place the FoodSmart here, beneath the window, along with the water dispenser and coffee-maker, so this little area becomes sort of like the galley. And then over towards the back, there...' she pointed towards the rear of the hold, where the large exit door was open and ramped down to the pad outside, 'we could put the toilet pod.'

Aaron nodded casually, 'okay, that seems sensible enough.'

'The passenger seats could be arranged in a rinky dinky semi-circle facing the other viewing window, and maybe we can install the toob in the middle of the seats. What do you think?'

Aaron shrugged, 'I guess, if you think that'll look nice.'

'Trust me, I know all about look-nice,' smiled Jez.

Ellie smiled. *Jez, the frustrated interior designer.*

Aaron got to his feet and walked across to where Jez had indicated where the FoodSmart would go, and studied the route the power cable feed would have to take, plus the feed-offs for the other powered utilities. Ellie watched as both of them discussed the best way to route the feed, and smiled with a belated sense of satisfaction.

She had wondered whether this odd little team of theirs would work out. She had considered Jez and Aaron to be opposites in many ways. Jez was loud, brash, extroverted, impulsive and impractical, and he in turn was laid back, quiet, sensible and very practical. Ellie had expected them to dislike each other on sight. Chalk and cheese. Maybe they had at first, but there seemed, despite a cautious wariness of each other, a growing mutual respect. She had expected friction, sparks even, but so far, thank crud, there had been none. Even the issue of Jez's small clothes mountain had been resolved painlessly. Instead of Aaron going ape when he'd seen what she had brought into the cabin from their recently abandoned cube, as she had thought he might, Aaron had simply found a storage locker in the cargo hold and had told her she could toss her things into that.

Ellie watched them as they walked along the metal wall, discussing, gesturing. It felt strangely like some new unorthodox family had been magically squeezed and shaped like clay, from the solitary forms of three lonely people. Jez and Aaron though, were more like an older brother and sister, than a mum and dad. It was an odd and comforting sensation that she savored as it pleasantly passed over her.

She lay down on the floor, propping up her head with one skinny hand as she finished off her bowl of Solar Nuggatz, Harvey sitting cross-legged beside her and chewing on his bowl of dry, brown protein pellets.

What a peculiar family we make, she thought.

CHAPTER 3

'So, for only four hundred creds you're getting a once in a lifetime trip up to the last arctic wilderness of this world. In ten, twenty years it'll all be gone.'

The couple stared at her in disbelief. 'We really have *snow* on Harpers Reach?'

'Oh yes! Thousands of square miles of beautiful virgin snow, untouched, unseen by any other humans.'

'I can't believe it. I thought it was all just orange mud and rock out there,' said the woman.

Jez spread her palms with shared disbelief, 'I know! It's amazing, isn't it? And this is *your one chance to see it*. We'll set down on the snow, and provided the O2 conditions are right, we can camp out overnight on it.'

'That sounds really rather primo. Wonderful. Four hundred creds you say?'

'Yes that's right, four hundred per person. That buys you four nights aboard the *Lisa*, a comfortable, spacious, pleasure cruiser with all the facilities you'd expect.'

'You have holovideo entertainment aboard?'

Jez smiled, 'of course we do…with all the usual channels.'

The man turned to his wife. 'Well?'

'Oh lumpkin, let's do it! It won't be around forever,' she turned to Jez, 'will it?'

Jez shook her head sadly. 'No ma'am. Before you know it, it'll all be gone forever. And this may be your only chance to see it for yourselves. There is no other shuttle service like this on Harpers Reach.'

Jez leant toward the woman, and looked cautiously around before adding quietly, 'and best to book now and enjoy it, before the unwashed plebs below catch on and ruin it,' she said nodding towards the plaza's balcony, and the city below. 'If you get my drift. Get it while it's *exclusive*.'

The woman nodded, 'I know what you mean,' she replied with a hint of distaste in her voice.

'Okay, so do we book a trip through you?' asked the man.

'Yes indeed. We can swipe your cred-card right now and I can then book you onto our next flight, which is scheduled to leave in five days' time.'

'Five days? Hmm that's a little short notice. When's your next trip after that?'

Jez pulled out a tablet and carefully scrutinized the complicated spreadsheet of data that scrolled down the glowing screen. She sucked in breath sharply and clucked uncertainly.

'Well now, hmmm. We're down to the last two seats for this next trip. That was full but we had a late cancellation, and then sadly, the trip after that is already fully booked-up.'

'Oh, well what about the trip after that then?'

Jez shook her head sympathetically, 'booked up as well, I'm afraid. Can I give you some honest advice?'

The couple both nodded eagerly.

'I'd take these last two spots for the next trip. I know it's short notice for you, but the way things are going, it could be weeks, even months before we might be able to get you up there onto that lovely snow. And you'd want to be one of the first to visit it, right?'

'Oh, yes,' said the woman. She looked at her husband. 'Lumpkin?'

'Okay, okay…let's have those last two seats. You will be able to get us on won't you?'

Jez nodded, 'yes, let's not waste any time though. One of the other girls on our sales team might book that slot if we're not quick enough.'

The man's eyes widened with a growing sense of panic. He hastily fumbled for his cred-card, pulled it out of his jacket and thrust it urgently at Jez.

Jez smiled, took it and deftly swiped it across the optical reader at the top of her tablet. 'And there's another fifty creds booking fee per person on top of that,' she added with a look of concern, 'regretful the cost of red tape in this damned city, isn't it?'

Neither the man nor his wife seemed to care too much about that as she totaled up the credit charge and processed it electronically.

'Well? Did we get those last two places?' the woman asked anxiously.

Jez looked down at the display, pleased that the *very first* two ticket sales she had just made on behalf of *Goodman Tours* had been such a cinch.

She offered them a sigh of relief, 'yes, it looks like you got there just in time. Lucky you!'

She handed them a printed slip. 'Here's your boarding details, and the time of departure. You'll need to arrive at least an hour before our departure time to be processed by the port authorities.'

'Oh lovely!' the woman replied.

'You two are going to have the trip of a lifetime,' said Jez beaming at them, her voice rich with warmth and sincerity, as if they had been friends for a lifetime. 'Just don't forget to bring some thick and cozy clothes.'

She bid farewell to both of them, and watched them walk away across Devinia Plaza towards a row of off-world jewelry shops.

Like taking candy from a baba.

She grinned.

Oh this is going to be so-o-o-o easy.

CHAPTER 4

The old man watched from afar. Watched Ellie Quin eating heartily, smiling, laughing, in good spirits.

Good.

He wondered if she had the slightest inkling yet; if her mind was telling her at a subliminal level, that there was something inside her, something so very important, something that would irrevocably change all of humankind.

Behind those delicate features, he wondered what this creation of his was really thinking about as she smiled and appeared to listen to the banter of her two friends. He studied the girl as her attention momentarily wandered and she casually cast a glance upwards to the sky. She was watching a stream of cargo tugs servicing a distant freighter hanging in low orbit.

Edward Mason smiled.

Yes, that's my little girl. Following her programming - dreaming of escape.

He knew that was what she must be thinking about. He knew that because he alone had engineered her very psyche; he had engineered that powerful nomadic desire into the very core of her personality. She was built to be that way. And for a moment, for a fleeting moment, he felt a shred of pity for his creation. For however long she lived, and it wouldn't be for too long, she would probably never know true contentment, she would never feel at peace with her environment, she would always be pushed by that basic, artificially enhanced urge to press on to pastures new.

You were designed that way, my dear. To want – to need - to travel. To spread your wings. No different really to the homing instinct of a pigeon. Or the up-stream desire of an Old Earth salmon to return to its breeding grounds. Programmed instinct.

He noted her attention returned to the animated conversation going on around her. Ellie's female friend looked to be a few years older, and the man, at least another ten years older. They seemed very close; a strong bond between the three of them.

Very interesting. She has managed to make friends.

Which was indeed curious. Mason had designed her to be introverted, shy, secretive; to find establishing relationships difficult. That was an important characteristic that had been built into her personality so that she would instinctively seek anonymity, obscurity - so that she would habitually avoid drawing attention to herself. That she would never have her instinct to travel compromised by a friendship; torn between moving on and leaving behind someone she'd grown attached to.

He had assumed that, when he finally caught up with her, he would find her utterly alone, without any friends at all. But it seemed that, to some extent, her personality had reached a little beyond its programming. *Very interesting. An example of nurture over-riding nature perhaps?*

Perhaps her parents had managed to teach her how to reach out and find friends. It was so fascinating. He smiled as he acknowledged that there was no way for sure that one can totally predict how a human life can develop. Despite her DNA virtually being authored from scratch, designed in a petri-dish, it appeared as if the environment of her childhood had found a way to change her, just a little.

What a fascinating creature you are, Ellie Quin.

He wondered, though, whether these two friends of hers would present a problem. It was hard to tell just yet. They could be a help or prove to be a hindrance. The time was coming when Ellie would need to be guided off this world and out into the universe to do what she was designed to do. There was always the remote possibility that the Administration had caught wind of this, and that even now, their agents might be en route to Harpers Reach or, worse still, be here on the planet already and beginning to close in on her.

He had been thorough in ensuring that nothing had been left behind him when he had faked his death in the upper stratosphere of Pacifica, and then disappeared. The extensive notes he had made on her in his personal journal had disappeared with him. All that had remained were his digital notes, locked away in that non-descript directory, and even then, he had been careful never - *never* -to reveal the name or whereabouts of his precious child.

He was certain the Administration had no conceivable idea of the fate that awaited them.

After so many years of patience, decades of patience, things were finally beginning to happen. The end of it all was in sight, and he was here to ensure that *his* little girl spread her wings and flew away with the minimum of fuss.

With, or without, her friends.

CHAPTER 5

Ellie awoke with a start. The soft chiming of the alarm beside her pillow had featured somehow in her dream. She vaguely recalled being chased by someone or something; fighting desperately to stay ahead of some closing threat behind her, clambering over rocks and rubble and all manner of unlikely obstacles to keep in front of it. The beep had been some sort of proximity warning coming from a device on her belt, urging her to go faster as it grew louder and more insistent.

'Go for it, girl,' Jez mumbled sleepily as she turned over in the cot above, and quickly fell asleep again.

Ellie rolled out of her bunk, pulled herself across the grilled walkway and leant against the sink on the opposite bulkhead. She splashed some cool water across her face.

It did the job. It woke her up.

She sprayed a cloud of ActiBacto under her arms, up her nightshirt to kill the sweaty-socks smell of the cabin that clung to her.

She looked up towards the front of the cockpit to see Aaron dozing in the pilot's seat, his large legs pulled up onto the arm of his seat, and his cap tugged down over his eyes. Through the windshield, looking forward, she could see the first light of day staining the purple sky with a hint of peach, and the drab ground below raced beneath them still bathed in the violet-blue shadows of night.

Their passengers would be waking up soon and it was Ellie's job to play the stewardess. Yesterday had been the first day of the four day trip. They had set off at midday to allow their ten paying guests the best light with which to see the spectacle of the port and the exterior of the dome of New Haven and, of course, the encrusted shantytown along the base of it. Ellie had joined them by the recently installed viewing windows in the hold and *ooohed* and *aahed* along with the rest of them. Second time around, it had been just as breathtaking to behold the sheer, awesome scale of the dome.

One of the older ladies confessed it had been several decades since she had last seen anything outside of the city. Ellie wondered how a person could endure living so long in one contained environment without at least stepping outside once in a while. Several uninterrupted decades trapped inside New Haven? She'd go mad.

Ellie had studied the ten passengers they had aboard as they gazed out of the window, watching the city begin to shrink as Aaron eased the shuttle away, heading northwards. There were three older couples, varying in ages from, she guessed, mid-forties to mid-fifties. Ellie had struggled to engage them in a little small talk, something that didn't come that easy to her, unlike Jez who could effortlessly exchange banalities with anyone, and somehow enjoy it too. Two of these couples had taken on the trip as an anniversary present to each other. For the third couple, the trip was a birthday present from the husband to his wife.

Then there were two brothers, both in their early thirties by the look of them. She had found out that they owned a holo-board advertising business between them. The older of the two, Sam, had proudly told her that thirty-six percent of the floating holographic billboards that floated around the city were theirs. It was a booming business he had assured her, and they were one of the biggest players in New Haven. In fact, Jez had actually been in the process of renting some billboard advertising time from them when she'd decided that Sam and his brother, Ryan, could do with a couple of tickets and a well-earned break from making lots of money.

Ellie shook her head and chuckled. *She never misses a trick.*

The other two passengers were each on their own. One was a young woman, Corin, perhaps a little older than Jez. Jez had referred to her as an *Airbag*. Ellie knew the stereotype well; young woman married to a richer older man, her own air car...usually one of the bigger, chunkier, utility models. Her type lived their lives entirely above the twenty-four storey mark, flitting from one tower-top boutique to the next. Corin was already flirting quite shamelessly with the two bill-board brothers, presumably enjoying the freedom of being off the leash and away from her sugar-daddy.

The last passenger was an old man, probably in his mid-sixties by the look of him. He hadn't said a great deal so far, but had gazed with an obvious pleasure at the chaotic comings and goings of vessels great and small from the port, and the intricate web of geodesic metal struts that lined the outside of the dome. Ellie suspected he was an old time colonist coming out one last time to see how much the world had changed.

She dressed quickly in the uniform that Jez had picked out for both of them to wear. For once it seemed Jez had been able to exercise some degree of restraint over her more flamboyant taste in clothing, and had selected some navy blue, form-hugging neoprene polo-necked tops, white miniskirts and navy-blue leggings for them to wear. She had also picked out some clothing for Aaron; crisp clean white slacks and a navy blue blazer with white braided epaulettes. But Aaron wasn't playing ball. He had resolutely refused to wear them, and showed no signs yet of weakening, despite Jez's constant badgering and nagging.

Ellie ducked and looked into the mirror beside the FoodSmart. She smoothed down her lank and lifeless mouse-brown hair and quickly applied a little liner and lipstick, still feeling a touch self-conscious at the thought of wearing cosmetics. She definitely enjoyed seeing her face transformed into something that looked prettier, more glamorous like Jez, but it still felt…bogus, like she was a child playing at being all grown up.

Ellie took several steps to the aft of the cabin, to a door in the bulkhead that led down into the cargo hold – now known as the *Passenger's Suite*.

She opened the door and let herself in. The glow strip on the ceiling was turned down, and most of the pale illumination in here came from the growing light of dawn streaming in from the two wide viewing windows.

Curtains…we'll have to install some curtains for the next trip.

She looked around the suite. She couldn't see anyone up just yet. The couches, arranged in a semi-circle facing one of the windows, were all closed and being used as individual sleeping pods. She tiptoed quietly in, walked silently across the carpeted floor towards the FoodSmart and started to prepare breakfast.

*

Aaron awoke from his fitful sleep as the smell of freshly made coffee drifted up into the cockpit from the hold. He also detected the savory smell of grilled fagurters and toasted wheat sheets. Ellie must be up already and tending to their guests, he decided. He stretched in his seat, his legs long enough to reach across and nudge the armrest on the co-pilot's seat next to him.

The jimp, curled up on the seat like a lap dog, stirred briefly and muttered something unintelligible and then was still once more. Aaron wondered whether the creature was dreaming. He wondered if *any* of the thousands of different models of genetic products out there actually dreamed. He cast a glance sideways at him....

Him?

Ellie's incessant campaign to *humanize* the jimp was beginning to take a hold. But it wasn't a good idea really. The jimp's license expiry was only a few months off. That was why Aaron had been able to buy him so cheaply. When it did expire, the pigment in the manufacturer's logo on his – *it's* - head would change color to red, and Harvey would very soon after curl up and die. Ellie was going to find that quite hard to deal with if she continued treating the thing like a surrogate child.

Aaron heard Ellie greeting one of the guests with a chirpy *good morning*.

He was relieved not to have to interact with the passengers. In fact, so far he hadn't once stepped back into the hold to meet any of them, despite a couple of polite requests from one of the couples to meet *the ship's Captain*. He really didn't envy Ellie's and Jez's role; having to mix it with them, cater to their every whim. Piloting, he had assured both girls, was a *full time* job, and even though the auto-helm was on the case most of the time, there needed to be someone on hand, in the cockpit, who could handle the vessel in case there was a problem.

He wasn't entirely sure they'd bought all that. But since it was *his* ship, *his* money they had spent converting her into a leisure barge and *his* loss if it all went belly up, he decided it didn't really matter if they did or not. He wasn't going to wear that damned uniform Jez had given him, and he doubly wasn't going to go back into the…*Passenger Suite*….and strut around like a pompous idiot to impress their paying guests and indulge in polite chitter chatter with them.

He'd feel like an utter moron.

Aaron was nervous that this whole enterprise was going to be found out for what it was by those people back there; a quick and corny cash-in. That some bright spark was going to notice that they'd been accommodated in a rusty old freight container, and the ship was nothing more than an ageing tug, splashed with white paint.

Still, so far so good. There had been no grumbles as yet, at least none that Ellie or Jez had reported. And, of course, he noted with a warm glow of satisfaction, the money was already tucked up safely in the bank; four and a half thousand creds of it already.

He settled back in his padded seat and felt the heat of the morning sun as it emerged with a fan-like explosion of rays over the mostly flat and featureless horizon ahead.

*

They approached the arctic line towards evening on the second day. They watched the distant, thin ribbon of white ahead of them slowly thicken as the shuttle hurtled towards it. Jez stood behind the pilot's seat and gazed, slack-jawed at the approaching spectacle.

'Oh-my-crud, this is in-cred-ible! I can't believe I'm seeing this with my own eyes!'

'Yeah, it's a breathtaking sight alright,' said Aaron.

'I mean, after days of seeing just so much orange mud…it's, like, I dunno…startling,' she continued. 'It's like the edge of the world, or something.'

Ellie came forward. 'Great isn't it?'

Jez, beaming, turned to her. 'Fregg, you know what Ellie? I'm so totally glad we met.' She grabbed her in a crushing headlock and planted a kiss on her forehead.

Harvey cocked his head inquisitively, whilst Aaron rolled his eyes and sighed. 'Sheeesh...let's ease up on the girly excitement and try and keep things professional back there, okay?'

Jez nodded, still smiling. 'Don't worry Aaron. They'll think I've been living out here all my natural life. I'm pretty good at *bluffing it*.'

She had suggested giving the passengers a little tour-guide routine; just some background spiel, a few facts, a few figures and an explanation of why it was all one day going to vanish - just enough that their customers felt like they were getting their money's worth.

'Okay so most of the detail is a load of crud I've looked up on the GEO channel, or made up, but fregg, they're not going to know, are they?' she said.

'Just as long as it *sounds* correct,' said Aaron, 'and they don't figure that we're a bunch of rank amateurs having our first go at this.'

Ellie placed a reassuring hand on his shoulder. 'Don't worry, Jez's good at razzing, they'll believe every little word of nonsense she tells them back there.'

'It's all crap,' Jez smiled and spun round on her heels. 'But I'll have them believing I'm an expert,' she muttered with a flick of her jet black hair, and making her way down the cabin towards the aft bulkhead door.

'Is she always so sure of herself?' asked Aaron.

Ellie watched her open the door and enter the passenger suite. 'Always.'

*

'Ladies and gentlemen, we are rapidly approaching this world's arctic shelf. If you care to look out of the viewing windows on either side…'

Most of the passengers had been staring lackadaisically at the toob, watching some imported off-world chat-show. With Jez's loud announcement breaking the fug of creeping boredom, the toob was instantly forgotten and all ten passengers crowded to either side of the suite to look out at the approaching spectacle.

Jez joined the billboard brothers, Corin, and one of the middle-aged couples in one window and stared out at the approaching ice sheet, now as thick as a thumb held out at arm's length. She had anticipated that the transition from non-arctic to arctic would have been gradual; starting with small patches of ice and snow that gradually grew in size and density. She couldn't have been more wrong. As they drew closer, hugging the dusty ground below them, she could see they were approaching a towering wall of ancient ice, several hundred feet tall. Its base was littered with shattered blocks of ice, a glittering rubble heap of shards and glistening faceted boulders of melting ice.

'As you can see, if you look at the bottom of the shelf approaching us, there is a lot of freshly broken ice. That's ice that has broken away from the shelf as it continues to melt and withdraw northwards.'

Jez had tried to find some information on the arctic region of Harpers Reach on the Toob- GEO Interactive channel. Despite a heroic effort on her part, she had found very little on it. After a long time patiently scanning through the lists of content, and being sidetracked a couple of times by a juicy celebrity gossip page, she had eventually found a menu devoted to natural history and a page of historic notes on the

Big Warming of Old Earth. Jez decided the facts and figures she pulled up there, dating from the first half of the 21st century onwards, were probably good enough to pass as data harvested from below.

'Detailed measurements taken here, over the last twenty years...'

Go on then girl, make it sound authentic and official.

'...conducted by the Colonial Bureau of Arctic Studies, have shown that the shelf is withdrawing northwards by three miles every year. That the ice-mass of the north polar region is decreasing by two-and-a-half percent every year, as the temperature of the planet warms up,' she announced, checking out of the corner of her eyes to see whether she was being given any skeptical frowns. Encouraged, she tried to remember some more of the little factoids she had read on the dying days of Old Earth's polar caps.

'If you look at the ice face itself, you'll see different layers of white and grey. That's where the density of the ice changes and is a reflection of environmental changes here on Harpers Reach from long before man settled on the planet. As you can see, there have been climate changes in the past, but this time round the warming will eventually melt all of it.'

'So why IS the world warming up?' asked the middle aged lady next to her.

Jez concentrated for a moment as she recalled the detailed explanation Aaron had given her a few days ago. Somewhat bored and irritated by his lecturing tone, she hadn't listened to all of it but, but she could recall enough of it to parrot-it-back.

'As the atmosphere thickens across the planet, thanks to the work of the Oxxon refineries right at the very top of the world, the surface heat of the ground, warmed by the sun, is then trapped beneath it. The atmosphere functions a bit like a one way mirror, allowing...'

Crud, technical words coming up. I hope I get this right....

'...*infrared* and *microwave* energy in one way, but not out the other. In effect, functioning like a layer of insulation,' Jez said, proud with herself that for a few moments there, she'd managed to sound vaguely like an egg-head, even if she didn't really understand the first thing of what she had just been saying.

The shuttle began to rise in altitude as the mottled white wall ahead of them loomed up large and intimidating. As the final thousand yards distance dwindled, the shuttle rose and dramatically skimmed over the top of the cliff with only a few dozen yards to spare.

Jez heard a collective out-letting of breath from either side of her. Ahead, the landscape was a brilliant, glittering, plain of white, punctuated here and there by enormous cracks and crevasses that snaked all the way to the edge of the arctic shelf. A world of orange and brown had suddenly been replaced with one of white, blues and subtle violets, in the blink of an eye.

She felt a passing surge of emotion that almost threatened the precise line of her lips. She wasn't sure what it was...pride, sadness, loss?...or perhaps a dawning glimmer of realization that she was privileged enough to see something so beautiful; something that would one day be little more than a footnote on some other planet's Toob-Interactive menu list.

As the doomed icy wilderness rushed past beneath them she felt like she was beginning to understand why Aaron and Ellie had spoken of it with a mixture of wonder and sadness. She decided to let their passengers enjoy the next few minutes in silence. She understood that what they could take in with their own eyes would mean far more to them than any hastily collated info-babble she could fill their ears with.

It was all a load of baloney anyway. Even Jez had to admit, there really were moments in your life when the best thing you can do is just shut up for a minute.

OMNIPEDIA:
[Human Universe: digital encyclopedia]

Article: 'The Legend of Ellie Quin' > The Eco-collapse of Harpers Reach

Several hundred years after Ellie Quin's death, Harpers Reach was once more a deserted planet; it became yet another cautionary lesson in how not to terraform a world.

The problem had been a miscalculation of the frozen water available. There simply wasn't enough to create a thick enough and sustainable atmosphere. The thin atmosphere that was produced, soon succumbed to the naturally occurring chlorine and sulfur seepage from beneath the planet's surface. A process that quickly eroded the already meager ozone coverage above the tropospheric layer.

Arguably, if the population holed-up in New Haven and Harvest City had been convinced to decamp from their protective domes earlier, once breathable air had become reliable enough, and had proactively cultivated the land with UV-resistant oxygen producing crops...they might have turned the tide and consolidated the planet's atmosphere in time to make it indefinitely sustainable.

This didn't happen though.

As the decades passed after the Oxxon refineries had closed down, the atmosphere gradually decayed to the point at which there was no longer a possibility that life could ever be led outside without the need of an oxygen mask. The one shot they had at turning the planet into a habitable world had been spent and wasted.

The two cities became over-crowded and conditions inside both domes eventually became unsustainable. When it became clear that Harpers Reach was unlikely to mature into a viable planet that could one day contribute to the economy of Human Space, trade links withered and commercial deliveries began to wane.

There are many varying accounts of the last fifty years of life on that planet. Some of these historical accounts are truly biblical and utterly grisly in their depiction of the final years. There are tales from New Haven of mass die-offs through suffocation and starvation. Tales of order breaking down and the city divided into various factions that fought viciously for the dwindling resources available. There are horrible tales of barbarism, butchery and cannibalism as the remaining, doomed city dwellers struggled desperately to survive against ever lengthening odds.

But these are all tales.

The world, of course, did eventually die; however, most of the inhabitants of the city migrated, as had those of Celestion, to other, better managed, colony worlds in the sector. A few of the more adventurous colonists remained on that muddy, orange world, enduring terrible hardship for several more generations, convinced that the world might one day be wrestled back under control. But records show the last of these isolated and tiny communities died off four hundred years ago.

Since then, as far as it is known, Harpers Reach has remained uninhabited by anyone. From time to time, archaeological parties have been known to fly down into the ruined city of New Haven in order to spend a few months wandering beneath the domed roof amongst the dust-coated towers and streets and the dark shells of tall buildings.

There are some wonderfully shot images of that place; poignant compositions of interiors that once were homes, of dust-coated cups and plates set for final meals that never quite happened, of shop fronts still open for business but containing nothing but ghosts of the past.

It is remarkable how much remains preserved, even to this day.

User Comment > Gallis234
Hey, I once did a dig there with the System History Circle. You know it's weird, the buildings are still standing. Like a giant ghost city. Very creepy place. See my instaweb page. Cool holos of it.

User Comment > Stay-at-home Monstuh
My mum sucks on goosti-gorkins when she thinks I'm not looking.

User Comment > Lebby-Chik890
Sucks 'em? She's doin' it all wrong Stay-at-home.

User Comment > Anonymous
Gallis, did you feel the eyes of the dead on you as you picked around New Haven? There was a holo-frightener on the old toob

about a bunch of kids visiting an old abandoned dome-city. Didn't end so well for the kids.

CHAPTER 6

Deacon looked out of the long and wide lounge window at the city below. New Haven was like so many other new world cities; untidy, overcrowded and garish. Every spare surface seemed to be filled with animated commercial images, the sky littered with floating billboards. It was one big, vulgar, tasteless bazaar that seemed to be poorly controlled by the city authorities.

It wasn't as if it even had any unique charm. There was nothing out there that was uniquely of this world, nothing that identified this city, this world, from hundreds of others like it. Most of the logos he spotted amongst the chaos of flickering, flashing, brightly colored graphics were ones that he had seen over and over again with monotonous regularity; the same old companies selling the same old rubbish to the gullible herds throughout Human Space.

It was totally homogenous, generic. New Haven was as instantly forgettable as most of the other cities he had visited in his life; a ramshackle bubble packed full of good little consumer-sheep, passively grazing on protein-poor fast food and gazing listlessly at all the holographic commercials.

He turned back round to watch Nathan Collobie - one of Mason's lab technicians - taking tissue samples from the bodies on the floor. Nathan was the ideal person to sequester from the Department of Genetic Analysis. He was a good technician; a very reliable and conscientious worker. But, most importantly, he already knew enough to be a security risk. It made sense then to continue using him, rather than bring in some other genetic technician to collect the tissue samples. The fewer loose ends Deacon was going to have to deal with when this was all over, the better. So, Nathan was along for the ride, like Leonard, until this little job was done.

Deacon watched as the technician worked. Nathan was in his late twenties and thickly-set. He wore fashionably baggy, bright colored clothes that sensibly blended in with the predominant fashion-paradigm on this world. He did a far better job of passing anonymously than Deacon did, with his distinctive dark tailored suit. He had to applaud the young man for that.

He moved with quick precision, producing a sterilized sampler bud from a hip-mounted pack and dabbing it delicately in the pool of blood beside the last of the four bodies splayed across the living room floor. He put the blood-tipped bud into a small plastic container, sealed it and then wrote the name and details on the lid:

Daniel R. Weston: biological father of candidate Imogen S. Weston.

He looked up at Deacon after he had finished. 'I'm done, I've got all of them.'

'Good. Add their samples to the others and have them sent back to the lab to be analyzed.'

'Yes sir,' replied Nathan casting another queasy glance around the room, the signs of their recent handiwork splashed in crimson across the walls and floor.

'Why don't you go into the kitchen and make yourself some coffee, Nathan?'

The technician nodded with obvious relief, and left the late Weston family's lounge for their kitchen. Deacon watched him go and felt some sympathy for both him and Leonard. This *was* an unpleasant business. But there simply wasn't the time to carefully take each candidate and its family's DNA and wait patiently for it to be deconstructed and thoroughly scrutinized before being able to press on and locate the next potential candidate on their list. They needed to be dealt with now. Unfortunately, doing it like this meant a few innocents would die along the way.

Deacon was now certain that Mason's creation was one of the names on the list; one of the sixty-three fetuses returned to Harpers Reach that Mason had personally been involved with. But he couldn't relax until he had *samples* from all of them, and their immediate relatives, taken back to the lab to study. Mason's handiwork would hopefully be in there somewhere, and once the candidate had been correctly identified, and he had made his report to the Administration that the child was dead...the crisis would be over.

However, there was always the chance that he'd made a mistake.

He could have picked the wrong world on which to start his search and the candidate even now, on the other side of the universe, might already be on the move, carrying out Mason's apocalyptic errand.

He just had to hope Harpers Reach was the right planet to have come to first. Certainly the city beyond this window was the kind of environment in which the candidate child might head towards to stay lost for some time. This place fitted the profile. If he were Mason, he would have almost certainly chosen a Paternity Request from this world.

He turned towards the three armed men standing silently near the doorway, awaiting his orders. 'Make it look like a robbery. Make a mess, break some things, take some things.'

The three men nodded and set about the task. The authorities in New Haven didn't amount to much more than a poorly organized, predictably corrupt, civic council. He could do anything he wanted in this city and their local law officers wouldn't be able to touch him, not after he waved his ID at them. But, for now, a little discretion would probably be wise. Time was of the essence, and he didn't want to waste any of it having to explain himself or confirm his supreme authority here to some local law enforcement monkey.

He watched the men as they coolly and systematically trashed the habi-cube, which Deacon had to admit, was one of the nicer abodes in this crappy little city, perched as it was, high atop one of the more desirable towers. And the Westons had seemed like such a nice family too, as he'd talked to them, introduced himself and politely asked if their daughter was home.

Pity.

He looked towards Leonard, who stared at a tray of crystal marbles that had been knocked off the coffee table onto the carpeted floor by Mr Weston as he'd fallen. The young lad's lips fluttered ever so slightly as he rapidly counted them over and over. That was how the young lad seemed to deal with situations he found unsettling; to focus on some tiny detail and quietly *quantify* it.

'Leonard?'

He looked up, muttering to himself, 'fifty-two marbles....fifty-two marbles, on the floor.'

'It's okay Leonard, all the nasty business is done here now.'

He nodded, 'yes, Deacon.'

'What name do we have next on the list?'

Leonard pulled out his data tablet. 'Quin, Ellie. We have details on a home address outside of the city, an agri-plot several hours away. But we have a logged entry into New Haven some months ago. Just the child on her own, not the family.'

'How old is the child?'

'Twenty. Turned twenty a few months ago. Deacon took several steps back towards the window and looked down at the city again.

Twenty...the onset of adulthood and this creature has come to the city all alone.

He turned to look at Leonard. 'What do you think, Leonard?'

The young lad nodded and spoke quickly, 'it could be her, it could be. It fits the behavioral profile we have produced - yes, at the first opportunity, running away from home to the nearest big city, a place full of people.'

'Yes,' replied Deacon thoughtfully, 'this one looks even more promising. Except we might be a little too late. If she's here in New Haven, she's already on the run.'

'But she may well be running *only* on instinct. Unless, of course, someone has told her that she *should* be on the run.'

'Yes,' Deacon replied thoughtfully. Leonard had a very good point. If she knew what she was already, if someone had sat her down and explained that to her, she might already be travelling under an alias. As it was, some months back she had boldly entered the city under her own name.

Careless. That was going to make it a lot easier to pin her down in New Haven.

'Leonard, we need to run her details through this city's transaction database, see where she buys her basics. We might even get lucky and find her name on some O2 bill, or a cube rental bill.'

'Yes Deacon. I'll get on it right away.' Leonard pulled out his tablet to begin the task. His eyes once more darted towards the body of Mr Weston, Mrs Weston, half her head sprayed across the family's gel couch, the two Weston children lying either side of the overturned toob projector on the floor...and the scattered marbles on the carpet beside them. 'Fifty-two marbles on the floor...fifty-two marbles,' he muttered unhappily.

Deacon gave him a reassuring pat on the back. 'Why don't you go and get yourself a coffee too, there's a good boy,' he said and then turned back to the window to look out once more.

Mason's abomination is out there somewhere.

This felt like the one. Dammit! He should have started with this one, this Quin child. The other seven candidates they had already visited and dealt with on Harpers Reach had all seemed so very normal, docile, quite unremarkable, just like the vast majority of the emotionally neutered masses out there.

'I think this Ellie Quin is the one,' he whispered quietly to himself.

It's her, all right.

CHAPTER 7

'It was a great success, Hufty. We landed on the snow in the late afternoon and our passengers loved it,' she said, then paused the diary as she looked out of the window.

She smiled at the recollection of them flooding out of the hold, down the ramp onto the snow like a class of unruly children. Later on, after the obligatory fun and frolics with snowballs, they had separated out, and wandered in couples and small groups around the arctic terrain. They had all carried emergency oxygen masks, but none were required.

As the light began to fade, Aaron had emerged self-consciously dressed in Jez's hand-picked captain's uniform and a thick, hooded coat over the top, more to hide his uniform, than to keep the evening chill out. He dutifully exchanged greetings and small talk with the passengers who were interested in the shuttle, about flying it and the topography of their world. And then, as the stars and the Veil emerged, and with the last trace of the sun finally absent from the sky,

Aaron had produced a metal crate and some packing fiber and started a bonfire that they all merrily huddled around as they stared up, entranced, at the purple night and the golden slash of the Veil.

And Ellie could have sworn there was a moment right then, a passing moment, when Jez glanced sideways at Aaron in his smart uniform and pursed her lips thoughtfully; giving some notion a fleeting consideration.

When they returned to the city two days later, and their passengers had disembarked to be processed through the port's immigration hall, the three of them had collectively heaved a sigh of relief. The whole trip had taken only four days and they had made a clear three thousand creds for their efforts, subtracting all of the overheads such as the fuel, food supplies and the docking fees at the port.

Ellie un-paused the voice-diary.

'Aaron gave both Jez and me the four hundred creds we agreed on, and another three hundred creds each as a bonus! *Seven hundred creds* for a few days work! We'd never find work that paid like that in New Haven if we spent the rest of our lives looking.'

Ellie paused the voice-diary again and set it down on the table. She sat back in the quilted couch and looked out of the restaurant window again at the passing street traffic. In the background, she could hear the Crazie-Beanie track being played. She tapped a finger against her cup in time with the beat and mouthed along with the gibbering Beanie catchphrase, whilst Harvey, sitting beside her, slurped a glass of protein-solution through a straw.

Jez was due to meet them for lunch, but true to form, she was running on Jez-time so was unsurprisingly late. She was out clothes-shopping, and Ellie knew she had probably completely lost track of the time and would show up an hour from now with some hastily concocted tale that would absolve her of any guilt whatsoever.

Ellie took a sip of her drink and then picked up the diary once more. 'The creds have been burning a hole in Jez's pocket since we returned. I'm surprised she lasted this long to be honest. I mean, it's been three days since we got back, and this IS her first shopping-frenzy. But she's being good. She's not spending it all.'

In one of her more lucid moments since returning to New Haven, Jez had handed

Ellie five hundred creds to look after for her, with the explicit instructions that no matter how much she pleaded and begged once *the fever* had gotten a proper grip on her, Ellie was not to give her any more of her money to spend. In fact, Ellie had banked that money, and most of hers, in one merchant's account. Both of them would need to be ID scanned for a withdrawal to be made.

She had kept out a hundred creds of her own money for spending too. She had weakened momentarily yesterday and taken herself down to Baldini's Bazaar to the stall in the main atrium on the ground floor where she had spotted those wonderful knee-high, turquoise pvc boots. Amazingly they were still there. So, successfully haggling the price down several creds, she had decided to treat herself. She ran a hand down the ribbed side of her lovely boots and smiled.

My little 'well done' present.

Ellie felt only the mildest pang of guilt for spending-out on them. She had worked hard on the shuttle trip; she had worked even harder painting the damned shuttle. The boots, therefore, were a well-deserved and belated thank you to herself for being such a good sport over the last few weeks.

'The plan was that we'd come back to New Haven and rest for a few days then do it all again. But there's been a change of plan,' Ellie said, struggling a little not to smile too much as she spoke.

'Aaron needs to take the shuttle across to Harvest City. There's a faulty component on Lisa that needs to be removed and a new one fitted in. According to Aaron it needs to be done over there because it's a lot cheaper...but also, there's another reason. He's going to see if we can extend the license on Harvey.'

She cast a glance down at him. The logo on his forehead was beginning to change in hue, very slightly...but enough to show that he was fast approaching the last few weeks of his life.

'The company that engineered him are also based there, so whilst he's in Harvest, he's going to apply for a renewed license, and an extender-serum.' She patted Harvey's bald grey head affectionately and he, in turn, looked up at her with his expressionless, beady black eyes.

'But the great news Hufty, the really great news, is that right on the flight path to Harvest City is home. Good old plot 451. He's going to drop me off, right outside the farm on the way there and pick me up on the way back!'

Ellie felt her cheeks flush with joy. Not only was she going back to spend a few days with her family, but Jez, curious to see what farming folk looked like, had invited herself along too.

She sighed. This was going to be a truly wonderful stopover. There was so much that she wanted to tell her family about and in turn, so much that she wanted to show Jez. Over the last few months, she had tried to explain to her what the farm looked like, how it worked, the sort of chores she used to do, what her Mum and Dad and Shona and Ted were like. But, she suspected, her confused gabbling had done little to enlighten her friend. Well, now she was about to see it all for herself. And, despite the fact that there wouldn't be a shop within several hundred miles, Jez seemed like she was genuinely looking forward to it.

Ellie looked out of the window once more, savoring the warm glow of satisfaction and contentment. She realized that she couldn't remember, *ever*, feeling this fulfilled, this happy. Even though she was still probably a year or two from having enough money to finally claw her way off-world and explore the great big universe out there, she was at last off the starting blocks and on the move towards that goal. And that's what really counted - that she was at last moving in the right direction. It was the standing still, the getting nowhere, that got her down.

She had a suspicion that many, many years from now, when she was an old woman she would look back at this moment. Sitting here, right now, in the window seat of this greasy-spoon chop-shop and looking out at the dreary tide of people passing by...she would one day realize that *this* was the moment when she knew for certain that it was all going to turn out all right in the end.

Savor the moment Ellie, savor it.

She nodded at the wise words of advice from herself. Dad had once said 'life goes by faster and faster with each passing year. If you get a chance to pause it every now and then, do it. Pause it, and just enjoy the view for a few moments.'

This, Ellie decided, was definitely one of those moments to pause.

It was then that she spotted a face in the crowd; a vaguely familiar face studying her intently from across the street. A moment passed as their eyes locked, and then the face disappeared behind a cluster of moving pedestrians and was gone, almost as if it had been erased by their passing. She sat up in her chair and pressed her face against the window, looking for it again.

There had been something familiar about that face, but she couldn't place it; a man, an old man, but gone now, like a puff of vapor blown away in a strong breeze.

'How odd,' she mumbled. 'Who was that?'

'Missss Eh-leeeee?' Harvey whispered quietly, looking up at her curiously.

'Oh it's nothing Harvey...I Just thought I saw someone I knew.'

*

Aaron checked the nav-display and shouted back over his shoulder towards the girls, 'it should be coming up any time soon ladies!'

Ellie and Jez scrambled forward to get a view as Aaron hit a button on one of the control panels and the windblast shields outside slowly wound up with a noisy whine. All three of them shaded their eyes and winced as the bright sunlight spilled into the cockpit. Below them was nothing but the ever-present orange clay mud, punctuated with sharp shards of rock.

'How far are we from Ellie's place?'

Aaron consulted a display, 'we should see it up ahead some time soon. That is, if I've got the right co-ords. It was plot 451, Ellie?'

'Yeah, that's right.'

Jez squinted. 'Hmmm, I see nothing but sand and rocks.'

'That's home alright,' Ellie shrugged. 'But we should see a large rocky outcrop soon.'

'Large? How large?' asked Jez.

'Well, not so much large….but big enough you won't miss it.'

They silently scanned the flat horizon racing towards them, and then finally Aaron spotted the slightest bump ahead of them. 'That it?' he asked, pointing.

Ellie smiled, 'that's it. The only thing close to resembling a hill in the area.'

'Okay here we go!' said Jez, 'a week on the ol' farm!' she announced with her rendition of a prairie accent.

'Crud, Jez, we're not that bad!'

'Just kiddin', farm-chik.'

Aaron dropped altitude by a hundred feet and they skimmed the ground. 'Here we go girls. You got your things ready?'

Ellie felt the strap on her shoulder. Her bag contained the presents she had brought from New Haven, her diary of course and the things she needed for the next few days. A change of clothes, toiletries, would all be at home, just as she had left them in her own habi-cube all those months ago.

'Yeah, we're good,' replied Jez casting a glance back at the three stuffed bags stacked by the bulkhead door.

Aaron looked down at the jimp, who was curled into a ball on the seat beside him, fast asleep. 'And you're taking your pet monkey with you?'

'Yes, he'll love it,' Ellie replied. 'So will Ted, for that matter.'

Aaron began to decelerate as the hill, Ellie's 'overlook', rushed forward to meet then. He pulled the nose of the shuttle up slightly as they slid gracefully over the top of it.

'And there it is,' said Ellie. 'Home.'

Jez looked out at the farm nestling at the bottom of the reverse side of the slope leading up to the rocky outcrop; three one-acre domes surrounding a smaller one in the middle. 'Hey, it's bigger than I thought,' said Jez.

Which was odd, because to Ellie it looked a lot smaller than she remembered.

Aaron eased back on the thrusters as they moved down the slope of the hill towards the farm. 'You did call them to let them know you were coming?'

Ellie shook her head. 'Nope. I want this to be a big surprise.'

Aaron nodded, 'well, a four hundred ton surface shuttle dropping out of the sky into their back yard unannounced...I think it'll be that alright.'

As the shuttle settled to the ground amidst a furious, amber dust cloud, Ellie spotted the round bulkhead door to one of the agri-domes swing open and a figure cautiously emerge holding a protective hand up to cover its face from the swirling eddies of airborne sand.

'Who's that who's just come out?'

It was hard to see.....a lean man for sure. 'My Dad, I guess.'

Aaron turned round to face them. 'Okay girls, I'm not going to cut the engines.'

'You're not? I'm going to get dust all over my hair,' Jez complained.

'So shoot me. Anyway, I'm not coming in for tea. I'm heading off now. I'll be back in four or five days for you, understand?'

Ellie nodded and then put an arm around one of his shoulders and hugged him. 'Thank you, for bringing me to see them.'

'Hey, that's alright,' replied Aaron awkwardly, taken aback. 'They deserve it as much as you do. Just make the most of your visit, eh?'

'I will do.'

Jez reached out a hand and punched his shoulder affectionately. 'Just don't lose the shuttle in some seedy poker game alright? I know what you trucker-boys are like.'

Aaron laughed, 'yeah right. And you mind your city-talk, Jez. There's little kids on that farm.'

'Don't worry, I'll have them swearing like troopers before we leave.'

Ellie gently prodded Harvey out of his slumber. He uncurled himself and dutifully followed her down the walkway as she made her way to the back of the cabin. Jez picked up the smallest of her three bags and Harvey, dutifully, the other two, much heavier, ones.

Ellie looked at her, then the jimp, 'poor little thing.'

'Just letting him earn his keep.'

They climbed out through the bulkhead and down the ramp to the ground outside, their eyes squeezed tightly shut against the swirling gritty clouds of blown up dust and the buffeting of wind. With a whine, the ramp pulled up and closed with a metallic clang. The shuttle swiftly rose a hundred feet into the sky and the turbulent air around them began to settle. Aaron banked the shuttle slightly to afford one last glimpse of them. They returned his wave. He straightened out once more and then headed northeast.

Ellie lowered her mask and took a sniff of the air. It was quite good today. She guessed one could be outside for a good two or three minutes before needing to resort to a mask. She then turned her attention to the figure standing motionless beside the bulkhead staring at her silently, intently, as the roar of Lisa's thrusters dwindled into the distance.

'Ellie?' said Jacob Quin. 'Is that you?!'

CHAPTER 8

'Dad,' she replied, her voice thick with emotion. Ellie ran forward and Jacob Quin swept his daughter up in his arms, holding her tightly.

Jez watched them as they held each other silently for a full minute. She looked anxiously around at the peach sky and the reddish ground, and then towards the round entry hatch leading inside to the agri-dome.

'Ahem, shouldn't we head inside before we all, like, suffocate?' said Jez, gazing uncertainly around at the infinite, flat horizon surrounding her.

Jacob Quin put down his daughter and Ellie turned round to introduce her.

'This is my friend Jez, you know, the one I told you about. She's lived in New Haven for quite a while, so she's a little fazed by not having a plastic sky over her.'

'Actually I'm a little fazed at being, like, outside? You know? Where there's no air?'

Jacob smiled. 'Yes of course, let's get you all in.'

He pulled open the hatch into the agri-dome and led them inside. He watched with amused curiosity as the jimp waddled past under the burden of Jez's wardrobe.

Inside, Ellie heard the voice of her Mum, Maria, calling through from some other part of their home.

'What the hell was that whooshing noise, Jake?'

Jacob winked at Ellie and then replied. 'Why don't you come and see?'

'Where are you?'

'Booster.'

They listened to approaching footsteps, and then, as she entered the dome, she cast a casual glance across the field of pulsating and twitching proto-meat bulbs towards Jacob. For a moment her expression was puzzlement as she studied the two people and the weird pale grey four-armed dwarf standing with her husband beside the exit.

'Oh-my-crud!'

Ellie smiled.

'Ellie! Is that you?! You look so different!'

Ellie realized she must do; her clothes, her hair –longer than it was when she left, the girly make-up. It had been nearly nine months since she had last seen them. Ellie realized she must look so different from the tomboy who had run out on them all that time ago.

Maria wiped her hands, smeared with engine oil, on a rag as she slowly approached her daughter, and then without another word said, she wrapped her arms tightly around her.

Whilst mother and daughter embraced, Jacob offered a hand to Jez. 'Pleased to meet you at last, Jez. Ellie told us you've been looking after her.'

Jez grabbed his hand. 'Well,' she replied coyly, 'she's done her fair share of looking after me too.' She looked around the dome and then at the rows of green gourds that wobbled and pulsated every now and then. 'Nice uh...farm, you've got here Mr Quin.'

'Thanks. It makes us money, just. And it's home too,' he replied. 'We like it.'

Jez wrinkled her nose.

'Ah yes. That's the meat crop, smells like spicy sweat doesn't it?' he said.

Jez nodded. That was a pretty good description.

Maria let Ellie go and introduced herself warily to Jez, studying the tall city-girl from head to toe as she did so. 'I expect Shona will love examining *your* clothes,' said Maria a little coolly.

Jez nodded and smiled awkwardly, 'great.'

Jacob called out for Ted and Shona. Ellie could hear the toob in the background, cartoons playing as usual. After being called another two times, they eventually wandered in unenthusiastically, before freezing in the doorway.

It was Ted who broke the tableau first and pointed at the jimp. 'Dad, look! An alien!!!!'

*

Supper was a stew made from the various vegetables they had growing in small patches wherever there was space in all three of the agri-domes, complimented with one of the meat gourds plucked from the soil in Booster, writhing and wriggling desperately until it was disemboweled, chopped into bloody cubes and added to the stew.

Afterwards, the Quin family and their guests sat out in the rec-area, the toob, for once, turned off and forgotten as Ted played with the jimp and Shona studied Jez in silent awe.

'So, how did you manage to afford to take a shuttle out here? I know those damned things are expensive,' asked Jacob, 'and what's more, I didn't know they made house calls.'

Ellie and Jez looked at each other. 'We're in business with the owner,' Jez replied.

'We do tours up to the polar cap,' added Ellie, 'Jez sells the tickets, I look after the passengers, and our friend, Aaron, flies the shuttle.'

Jacob nodded, impressed. 'And you make money doing this?

Jez was about to reply that they made a *lot* of money, well, off the first run they had anyway. But Ellie, sitting next to her on the hammock, subtly nudged her and answered instead. 'We do okay on it.'

She knew Mum and Dad were struggling a little right now as they crossed over from tubweed to this new meat crop. The last thing she thought they'd want to hear would be Jez bragging shamelessly about how much money she managed to extort from their passengers on their first sightseeing trip.

'Uh…yeah, it pays us enough to get by,' Jez added, 'better than the job I was doing when Ellie and me first met.'

'Oh, what was that?' asked Maria.

Ellie answered quickly, 'Jez used to work as an…*entertainer*.'

'Ooh, that sounds good.'

Shona's interest was piqued. 'Like on the toob?'

Jez looked uncertainly at Ellie. 'Not really, Shona,' she replied hesitantly.

Ellie decided a well deployed distraction was in order. 'So Ted, what do you think of Harvey?'

Ted turned round and grinned. 'He's great. I'm teaching him to play stone-paper-scissors.'

'Who's winning?'

'Well he is. He keeps using all four of his hands.'

Jacob studied the jimp for a moment. 'So is that *your* animal, Jez?'

'Oh no, Mr Quin. That's Aaron's, our partner in the shuttle business. He bought it cheap to help us with fixing up the shuttle. It's a strong little chap. It's taken a shine to Ellie though.'

Jacob had noticed the sinewy strength in the creature's four arms. He guessed any one of those four muscular limbs could do a lot of damage. 'It's safe isn't it? I mean, Ted playing with it like that?'

Ellie nodded, 'Harvey's very docile. Gene-imps are engineered to be that way.'

Jacob smiled. 'Harvey? Didn't you have an imaginary friend called that, when you were Ted's age?'

Ellie felt her cheeks color slightly. *Thanks for that Dad.*

Jez giggled and nudged Ellie. 'Oooh, I'm looking forward to hearing all these teeny-weeny baby stories about you Ellie-girl.'

'No Dad, he was called *Hufty*, not Harvey.'

The jimp looked up from the game with Ted. 'Name....issss....Har-veeeee.'

'Yes that's right Harvey, that's your name...not Hufty, Harvey.'

He nodded and Ellie thought she saw the flicker of a smile touch his lipless mouth.

'Well, it's getting past your bedtime Ted,' said Maria.

Ted thumped the ground angrily with his fist. 'Ohh Mum! Can't I stay up a bit longer?'

'No, come on. It's past your bed time as it is.'

'But I want to see Ellie.'

'She'll be here tomorrow when you get up, don't worry.'

'Can Harvey sleep with me in my cube tonight?'

Ellie glanced at her parents. They looked unsure about the idea. 'Maybe tomorrow night Ted,' she replied. 'We'll see how you and Harvey get on tomorrow, okay?'

Ted nodded sullenly as he got up and wandered over to the hammock to hand out kisses and hugs, whilst Maria gathered up his toys and took them across to Ted's habi-cube.

'I've really missed you, you little nugget,' said Ellie, squeezing him tightly and ruffling his tufted blonde hair.

'Me too. Are you staying here forever now?'

Ellie shook her head. 'Just visiting for a few days. But I'll be back again, and again.'

'Okay,' he said, satisfied with that, and then stood in front of Jez with his arms outstretched and his lips puckering. Jez was taken by surprise, expecting a timid handshake at best.

'No one gets away without a Ted-snuggie at bed time. Except Shona, that is,' Ellie explained.

'Thank crud for that,' Shona muttered.

Jez leant forward and awkwardly reached out for him. Ted wrapped his arms around her neck and planted a quick and self-conscious kiss on her cheek. 'You're a baby-babe,' he said with a nervous giggle.

Jez looked up. 'Is that good?'

'It means he's got the hots for you, Jez,' laughed Ellie.

'If he starts trying to impress you with armpit farts, then he's *really* hot for you,' added Jacob.

Maria returned from Ted's cube and peeled him off Jez. 'Come on then tiger-Ted, time for bed.' She led him away, with Ted waving over his shoulder as he staggered tiredly towards his cube.

The evening drifted on pleasantly.

Maria returned with the all-clear that Ted was fast asleep, Shona went off to her cube and returned dressed up in the most fashionable of her clothes for Jez to inspect and pass approval on. Ellie watched her friend with growing affection as she took Shona on and they exchanged tattle on clothes and accessories; Shona trying on Jez's hip bag and leather belt, and Jez some of Shona's play-jewelry.

Later, after Shona had gone to bed Jacob Quin opened a bottle of home-brewed wine which Jez admitted was quite nice after the first startling mouthful.

Ellie was grateful that her parents didn't cross-examine Jez, satisfying themselves with general questions about New Haven and what it was like to live there, which they both answered in turn.

Mostly honestly.

CHAPTER 9

The next day, Jacob Quin took the girls on a tour around the farm. Ellie was keen to see how well the meat crop was coming along, to be satisfied that, second time around, her father's attempt to grow them wouldn't end in another unpleasant bloodbath.

'So, what are they like to grow? Are they easier than tubweeds?' asked Ellie.

Jacob looked out across the acre spread of fidgeting meat-bulbs. 'Yeah, I think so. The big thing to get right is the temperature and humidity in here, which, thanks to Sean's Dad, we got nailed pretty quickly. The growth period is only four months from planting to harvest. We can get three yields per dome, per year from this.'

'That's great.'

'So, we've only set up Booster to take these...and we'll see how it goes. If it goes well, then I think we'll turn over Betsy and Buttball to them.'

'Have you still got tubweed set up in those two?'

'Oh yeah.'

Jez arced one of her eyebrows inquisitively, 'tubweeds?'

'Ahh, the curse of my life, those horrible things. You want to meet them?'

Jez shrugged. 'I've heard so much from you about them, I feel I know each and every one of them intimately.'

Jacob and Ellie exchanged a grin, and then he led the girls through to Betsy, Ellie's old agri-dome. In the moist warmth of the dome, the tubweeds swayed in silent shoulder high ranks before them.

'So what is it with tubweeds that you didn't like?' asked Jez, recalling on numerous occasions Ellie cursing the memory of those plants.

'Their attitude.'

Jez looked confused. 'Attitude? They're plants aren't they?'

'Originally they were an alien species of plant. But not entirely plant. Think of them as being half plant, half animal,' said Jacob. 'They *do* have just about enough intelligence to have an attitude.'

'And their attitude towards me was sheer malice,' added Ellie. 'It's mutual, by the way.'

Jez, curious, walked towards them, 'so what exactly can a malicious plant do to you then?'

'You get any closer and you'll see for yourself,' cautioned Ellie.

Jez stopped, and then advanced very slowly, one step at a time. The tubweeds nearest her swayed gently backwards as she approached them, wary of the unfamiliar scent. She was amused at their movement. 'Hey, that's so weird...cowering plants. I guess they're afraid of me by the look of it.' Jez suddenly lurched forward and raised her arms, 'boo!'

The closest tubweeds recoiled backwards with a spasmodic jerk and they heard a wave of rustling leaves ripple across the field in response. She chuckled and turned back to Ellie and her father. 'You could sell these as like...'stress plants' back in the city, couldn't you? You know, if you've had a really daggy day at work and want to take it out on something...just have one of these sitting in the corner that you can scare the crud out of.'

'I suppose that's an idea,' replied Jacob, 'but the problem is-'

One of the tubweeds nearest to Jez decided it had cowered long enough and that she wasn't the threat it had thought she was.

With a fast and graceful sweep of its pod it swiped Jez across the back of her thigh.

'Ouch!' she yelped and jumped backwards. 'I've just been fregging goosed by a goddamned fregging plant!'

Jacob looked down at Ellie with a look of surprise.

'Yes,' said Ellie, 'she can occasionally curse like a trucker,' she confided quietly with an apologetic glance up at her father. He shook his head and smiled in a way Ellie figured was tacit, unspoken approval.

Jez rejoined them, rubbing her leg. 'I can see why you weren't so fond of these psycho things.'

'Ted and Shona have no problem with them. It was only really Ellie that had this ongoing grudge-match with them,' said Jacob. 'I think it's to do with height though. They're the same with me, pull back every time I walk past them, but not Maria who's shorter than Ellie. I think they view anything tall as potentially threatening.'

'And probably your smell, Jez,' added Ellie. 'No offence, but they don't know your odor yet. In fact, you'll smell unlike anything they know - coming from the city an' all.'

Jez looked hurt. 'I smell….*urban*?'

'No,' she laughed, 'but you wear perfume, don't you? They've never encountered *Candique* under-arm before. They're probably petrified by the smell,' Ellie added with a wink and taking a few steps towards them, 'but me, they'll probably still remember my smell and damn well go for me, like they used to.'

As she tentatively approached them she warily watched the pods of the nearest plants for the telltale pullback; the indication that they were making ready to lash out. But instead the plants reacted in the same way as they had to Jez, cautiously leaning backwards, away from her.

'I'll be…' she muttered. 'They're scared of me too.' And then, she recalled one of the last things she had done on the way out of the dome all those months ago; her final act of revenge.

They remember that alright.

'Oh, there's something I want to show you Ellie,' said Jacob. He headed towards the exit hatch. 'It's outside.'

He grabbed a couple of O2 masks off the hook beside the hatch, handed them to the girls, then unclipped the one he wore habitually on his belt. 'It's not a great oxygen day today, so we'll take the masks.'

When they had fitted them on he quickly opened the hatch and ushered them through, closing it swiftly once they were outside.

'So what is it, Dad?' asked Ellie.

'Something that's long overdue. I managed to buy another primer a few weeks ago.'

'Oh, that's great Dad, well done you!'

Jez looked at both of them, confused.

'Sorry Jez, it's a part for our Cat,' Ellie explained.

Jez nodded uncertainly, 'o-o-okay, is it feeling better now…your cat?'

Jacob laughed realizing Jez still didn't have a clue what they were going on about. He took a few steps along the edge of the dome towards a sheet of dust-coated canvas draped over something large. With one theatrical gesture he grabbed the bottom of the sheet and pulled it away, revealing a weathered old caterpillar-tracked vehicle.

'The cat,' he announced.

'It's been out of action for quite a while because we couldn't find…*afford*, a particular part,' said Ellie. 'Not having the cat working has been a real drag, hasn't it Dad?'

'Yeah, you're pretty limited out here if you can't get around.'

Ellie walked over to it and looked in through the plexiglaz blister at the cabin inside. 'It's been a while since I've driven this old dear,' she said ruefully.

Jez was impressed. 'You can drive it?'

'Of course, it's not difficult really. Any old gumby can drive one of these things, even me.'

*

'Why can't we go too?' Ted and Shona chorused together.

'Because you're too young to be going out there without us,' Maria explained patiently, 'and Ellie and Jez don't want to have to be babysitting you both.'

Ellie nodded. 'Sorry guys. I'll take you for a spin when we come back.'

It had been her idea to take the cat and drive across to the old abandoned weather station a couple of hours away. It was a trip the family had done several times together, before the cat's primer had died on them, that is. The old weather station was one of the first colony outposts on Harpers Reach and had been finally abandoned over two hundred years ago. Ellie found it a fascinating environment to explore; the old metal hulls of prehistoric habi-cubes were welded together into a fascinating maze of dark, dungeon-like corridors and chambers. Much of this dark, forbidding structure was still in a robust condition. She thought it might be fun for Jez to take a look. After all, they had been inside the farm for three days now with only one brief trip outside to walk up the hill to her overlook to see the distant shimmering top of New Haven's dome. She suspected Jez was getting cabin fever.

For that matter, so was she.

The trip would be a nice antidote for them both, a chance to see a bit more of the desert wilderness of the planet, but mostly, Ellie decided, to provide her guest with some merciful relief from Ted's clinging adoration and Shona's incessant questions about the city.

'Is Harvey staying behind?'

Dad had suggested they take Harvey too. He wasn't sure about Ellie leaving the creature behind unattended with Ted. Ellie had failed to completely convince him that Harvey was utterly harmless and incapable of doing any damage to someone else. She could understand that. Looking at Harvey's arms, one could see there was a powerful strength in there, after all, jimps like Harvey were designed for very heavy labor, construction work.

Anyway, she decided, it would be a nice little excursion for Harvey too. 'I'm sorry, he's coming with us.'

Ted's face began to crumple with frustration and disappointment.

'Not fair, not fair,' he whimpered.

Ellie looked across at Shona, who also looked disappointed. For a moment, she was reminded of those poor children living out their lives up at the Oxxon refinery, isolated and bored. With only the toob to remind them that there was a world beyond the small bubble of their lives.

She decided now was as good a time as any. 'Look, I got you two a little present. I was going to give it to you tomorrow when Jez and I go back to New Haven, but I guess I could give it to you now.'

That stopped Ted's whimpering instantly, and Shona looked up with guarded interest. Ellie fumbled in her jacket pocket for it. She had kept it there, zipped up inside since she had bought it, sealed away from any moisture. Her fingers probed the little pocket and felt the hard, rough nugget within. She pulled it out.

'This is for you guys.'

Ted looked at it. 'It's a stone.'

'No it's not. It's a podkin.'

'A podkin!' yelped Ted.

Shona came forward. 'Oh, I know what those are! I saw an ad on the toob for them. It's a little creature you grow in the ground, isn't it?'

'That's right Shon'. You put it in some soil, water it and it will grow and grow some more, until it steps out of the soil. And then you've got a little pet for a month or so.'

Ted reached out for it and turned the brown lump over and over in his fingers. 'Cool,' he muttered staring at it, the trip on the cat forgotten for now.

'You can share looking after it,' Ellie added.

The distraction seemed to have done the trick, as both children hurried off to find a spare patch of unoccupied soil in Ted's dome, Booster, without stopping to say farewell.

'Come on then Jez,' she said, 'we might as well head out whilst the going's good.'

'Roger that, ' she replied.

'You're going to camp out there overnight?' asked Maria.

'Maybe. We're taking something to eat and drink and some sleep-sacks, and then we've got the option if we want to,' replied Ellie with a grin. 'It's been a while since I last camped out there.'

'I know, be careful though.'

'We will.'

'And if you stay there tonight, you'll be back tomorrow morning?'

'Yes...early. We're expecting Aaron to arrive with his shuttle later on tomorrow to take us back home.'

Home. Ellie winced slightly at using the word in front of her parents. It wasn't as if that city felt like home anyway. If any particular place felt anything like *home*, it was the cramped confines of Aaron's shuttle, oddly.

She leant over and kissed her mother on the cheek. 'See you later Mum.'

'See you Ellie, honey.'

Jez nodded politely to Mrs Quin as they stepped out of the central domestic dome into Betsy. As they passed the tubweeds, the plants leaned warily backwards from them and both girls had a giggle spooking them by lunging forwards. Harvey studied the plants silently, cocking his head on one side as he watched them sway.

Jacob Quin stood beside the exit hatch, one hand on the lever. 'Just go easy on her.

She's working fine right now, but she's an old cat that needs treating with a little love and respect.'

'I know Dad.'

'I've put in another Navset-beacon, just in case.'

Ellie nodded, 'we'll be alright. If we're not back later on today, we'll see you for breakfast tomorrow.'

He smiled, 'okay. You two have fun exploring the ruins.'

The girls each grabbed a mask from the pegs and put them on, Ellie fixing the mask onto Harvey's face for him, and Jacob pulled up the locking lever and swung the door open. They stepped outside and Jacob, with a little wave, quickly swung the door closed again.

If Ellie had known that the fleeting smile from her father as he swung the door to was the last time she would ever see his face, she would have said something more meaningful to him.

'See you later, Dad.'

CHAPTER 10

The ruin of the weather station was a two hour cat-ride away, approximately sixty miles south of the farm. There were about a hundred and fifty of these old abandoned outposts dotted across the planet, dating from the world's earliest inhabited days, long before either New Haven or Harvest City were constructed.

The cat rolled across the featureless landscape at an unexciting thirty miles an hour. Inside the cockpit, Ellie steered the vehicle in a relentless line, straight south.

'So, what do you think?' asked Ellie.

'Of what?'

'I dunno, everything.'

'Your family are nice, Ellie,' Jez admitted a little enviously. She felt like blurting out that she had never known hers and that she would have given anything to have had a childhood, to have had a family just like Ellie's.

'I really like them,' Jez added after a few moments. To Jez they seemed like a different breed, almost a different species, to the sheeple that filled New Haven. They seemed more alive, more alert, more friendly...more going on inside them than the dittoheads back in the city. She wondered if she were Ellie whether she would have had the strength of purpose to leave such a warm, embracing environment behind.

'What do you think of the farm?'

'Bigger than I had imagined,' Jez replied. 'I was expecting something a little smaller, crumpled and battered I suppose. It's a good home Ellie, you're lucky to have that.'

They drove on in silence for a moment before Jez added, 'I can see why you're not a big fan of those damned tub-thingys, though.'

'Yes, the curse of my life, those things were. I'm glad Dad's changing the crop over at last.'

'Kind of gross those gourd things, aren't they? I got to say, I nearly couldn't eat supper last night after I saw your Mum pull one of those things kicking and twisting out of the ground, and then butcher it right there in front of me in the kitchen.'

'Hmm, yes, but then that's natural food for you I suppose. A long time ago, people used to actually eat dead *animals*.'

'Eeeeww,' said Jez pulling a face. 'That's utterly grotesque, thank you Ellie-girl. All I can say is thank crud for protein-paste.' Jez looked out at the barren terrain ahead of them. 'So…you've been to this weather station before then?'

'Oh yeah, quite a few times. Dad used to take us kids there. It's great to explore and really fascinating to see how colonists used to live here in the early days.'

'Do you know much about that?' asked Jez.

'What the early days?'

'Yeah.'

'Sure. I studied colonial history for one of my citizenship modules. It was rough back then Jez, really rough. They had to make it on their own. There were no regular trade routes delivering essentials. Whatever they needed to survive, they had to produce themselves.'

'A bit like your family.'

'Maybe, but they had it much worse. They didn't have a city they could run to if things went wrong.'

'True,' replied Jez.

'It sometimes amazes me how so many people can allow themselves to become totally dependent on others to provide what they need,' said Ellie after a while. 'Take all those people living in New Haven, living on top of each other, all needing oxygen, water and food. But what would they do if, just for a few days, the food, the water and the oxygen supplies stopped arriving?'

'I dunno. They'd be alright for a few days, I guess. I'm sure the city has stocks of essential things put aside, just in case something like that happened.'

'You think so? But what if a few days turned into a few weeks?'

Jez thought about it for a moment. 'Hmmm, they'd be all in deep hooey, I guess.'

'Yes. It's something I've thought about since moving to New Haven….how vulnerable everyone is in there. And I wonder if it's the same on other planets? How many people across Human Space know how to do something as simple as find water? Or grow food?'

'If they're anything like me, not many,' replied Jez. Ellie had a point. Even here on this frontier world where the planet had yet to be properly tamed and the people living here were supposed to be of a tougher sort, resilient, capable of looking after themselves - the vast majority of citizens crammed into

New Haven wouldn't last a day without their regular StarBreaks meal and a bottle of sugary pop. If for some reason the freight ships suddenly stopped arriving, it would be a matter of only days before the citizens of New Haven started hungrily biting chunks out of each other, whilst Ellie's family could carry on quite happily…eating their freshly grown vegetables and meat gourds.

'I really want to get the fregg off this mud ball,' said Jez after a while.

'Me too,' replied Ellie.

'If we can make as much money as we did last time, crud….we could have enough within two years to get out of here.'

'If you can avoid spending it, that is.'

Jez reached both of her hands out to playfully throttle Ellie. 'Ach!! What are you, my mother all of a sudden?'

Harvey stirred at the sudden movement and watched Jez with intense eyes for a moment, before realizing the gesture was harmless.

'Oooh, did you see that?' said Jez, 'your monkey thought I was going for you.'

Ellie patted Harvey's head, 'who's a good boy then? Knows exactly who's boss, right?'

They rode in silence for a while, Jez fidgeting after a while like a bored child.
'Question for you, Ellie.'
'What?'
Jez hesitated, sucked air through clenched teeth. Ellie knew her noises well enough to guess it might be an awkward question.
'You....and Aaron,' she started, 'so have you.....?'

The question hung in the space between them, incomplete, waiting for Ellie to join some dots. And belatedly she did. Her cheeks turned crimson.

'Freg! What? No! God, no!'
'Hey,' Jez shrugged. 'He's not so gaga now I've tidied him up a bit.'
'Jez! He's...he's almost as old as my dad!'
'Hmmm...not by a few years. And actually, you're dad's not bad for his age.'
'Jez!'
'I mean it. He's lean...tidy, not all bloated by proto-lard sizzle snacks like most of the homs in New Haven.'
'Jez! Not my dad, please! That's totally grosso!'

Jez laughed and gently punched Ellie on the arm. 'Messin' with you, farm-chik. Just messin'. He's out of my goldilocks zone by about five years anyway.'

Ellie made a face. 'Thank God for that.'
'Aaron though...'
She turned to look at Jez. 'Seriously?'
Jez grinned. 'Much longer...and I'll be down to using something with a battery.'
Ellie closed her eyes and shook her head. 'I can't believe I brought you back home to meet my family.'

CHAPTER 11

Deacon watched the arid world pass by below. It really was an incredibly dull and ugly landscape, and from what he had seen in the few weeks he had been down on Harpers Reach, it was the same dull and ugly landscape right the way across the entire planet, with no significant features to speak of to break up the monotony. He could almost understand why ninety-nine percent of this world's population had crammed themselves into New Haven and Harvest City and refused to come out.

The shuttle he had appropriated from the New Haven authorities - with no explanation whatsoever and a mere flourish of his credentials - was pitifully old and slow. He guessed this shuttle had seen active service on several other worlds before this one; bought in second-hand by the planet's local law enforcement for the occasional bit of policing outside of the city.

Inside the main cabin, sitting on benches facing inwards, his team looked almost as bored as he felt. Leonard was busy scribbling on a tablet, his mind a million light years away, fraternizing with some mathematical distraction. Nathan sat beside him trying to watch his portable holotoob. He flipped distractedly from one station to the next, glancing momentarily at a steady procession of day time sopa-drams and home-shopping channels; nothing seemed to be holding his interest for long.

Deacon suspected the technician was suffering a mild form of post-trauma stress. Up close he'd witnessed those families butchered right in front of his eyes. The administration's dirty work carried out with ruthless precision and efficiency. He acknowledged there was once a time that he would have been equally horrified at the sight of children, women being gunned down in their own homes.

What has been done, has been done out of necessity.

And then there were the three hired guns. They sat in silence, two of them appeared to be asleep, the third gazed wearily out of one of the windows at the passing terrain. Professionals, mercenaries....each of them had been used many times before by the Administration to do its most grisly work. They were functioning on only the minimum amount of information required. Like bloodhounds, all three of them had been given the scent of Ellie Quin, and nothing more.

When this job was done, they too, like the two younger men sitting beside them, were loose ends that would need tidying up. When this job was done, there would be only Deacon heading back to Liberty on a star ship to make his report to the committee.

So far, seven candidates and their families had been eliminated. On one unfortunate occasion, a couple of hapless passers-by who had been unlucky enough to witness one of these executions: altogether a body count of about thirty people by Deacon's reckoning.

By the time he had gone through the complete list, he guessed approximately another fifty or sixty lives would have been terminated. When the last name on the list for this world had been eliminated, and the DNA samples collected, Deacon would take them back to the Department labs alone and have each sample analyzed in detail. It wouldn't take long to spot which of them was the handiwork of Doctor Mason.

Deacon had a strong feeling about this particular one though. The girl, Ellie Quin, had come from strong genetic stock. Studying the notes on the Quin Paternity Request, both parents had robust genetic profiles, with little or no evidence of regression or chaotic mutation, something of an increasing rarity in itself these days. Putting himself in Dr Mason's shoes, Deacon would be looking for a well matched and healthy pair of gene sets like those of the parents, Jacob and Maria Quin. Their child would need to be healthy and fit, and unimpaired by any kind of physical frailty. They were good starting stock for Mason to work from.

Deacon had hoped to find her quickly enough in the city. Her ID card, and transactions used against that ID, had helped him narrow down the area in which she was living. It was only when she had set up a merchant's bank account, in the last few days and used the address of a tenement tower in the Service Sector, that they'd been able to instantly zero in on her.

But the clever girl had already fled by the time they got there.

They had found the habi-cube empty. Deacon and his team had trawled through the things that had been left behind; some clothes, some very cheap furniture, and a sink full of food-encrusted washing up. He guessed from the detritus lying around that the Quin girl had been sharing with another female. Whether they had both left and gone their separate ways or gone together, he didn't know.

He wondered whether this child had been smart enough to realize she was already being hunted and had consequently fled. Or perhaps someone had informed her that the Administration's *bloodhounds* were closing in on her? But he couldn't think who.

Maybe Mason hadn't acted alone?

The thought was a concern. It wasn't beyond the realm of possibility that Mason had prepared the way for his child, had agents of his own out in the field watching over it, to ensure its safety.

Or maybe you're just jumping at shadows.

Deacon smiled and nodded his head. He was jumping unnecessarily. The Quin girl most probably simply run out of money and been forcibly evicted. It was just bad luck on his part that they had arrived a few days too late to catch her then and there.

He censured himself for thinking that Mason had his own army of like-minded agents out there. The man had been a lone crackpot. All the evidence so far had pointed to the fact that he had been working in isolation. And as far as he knew this Ellie Quin was alone, and more than likely unaware that there was anything special about her.

After finding her empty cube in the city, Deacon had consulted the immigration data file on Quin and noted there was a family address; a remote farm located on plot 451.

And where would an evicted girl with no money head? Home, of course.

The pilot broke the protracted silence in the cabin and Deacon's meditation.

'Sir?'

'What is it?'

'We're approaching the destination now, sir,' the pilot replied, pointing towards what looked like a shallow hill ahead of them, 'just beyond that spur.'

Deacon nodded and turned round to face his team. They were alert now. The mercenaries who'd been cat-napping were wide awake and Leonard, off wherever that mind of his took him, was back with them now.

'Alright we're here. It's a small domed farm. There are four other inhabitants including our target. Same drill as the last one....I want to be sure our target is there before we eliminate any of them. If the target is not, then we'll need someone alive to tell us where it might be, understand? So no-one fires until I say so.'

The mercenaries nodded in silence.

As the shuttle passed over the low spur, he saw the cluster of enviro-domes below; a humble, isolated smallholding. With one glance at the dust-covered plastic domes and the clutter of recycled machinery spare parts outside, Deacon already knew what the people inside were going to be like; good, hardy, colonial folk.

Pity.

'Alright, let's get this over with,' he barked over the whine of the engines.

CHAPTER 12

Ellie watched the shimmering sun drifting almost perceptibly downwards towards the flat horizon resting, it seemed, on an undulating bed of flaming oil. The shadows around the abandoned weather station lengthened and darkened as the evening drew in.

It seemed like nothing had changed since she had last been here two years ago. The same wind-worn forms of various cabins and modules, that represented one of this world's first communities two centuries ago, remained untouched and unvisited.

They were standing in the middle of the colony's greenhouse, a pyramidal structure of reinforced plastic panels that had been scoured by two centuries of airborne sand to a state of foggy, semi-opacity. Part of the structure had collapsed in the distant past. One of the sides of the pyramid had dropped down inside, leaving the other three sides still standing.

Ellie was fascinated by the shriveled, almost fossilized remains of the crops that had once upon a time grown here. Still standing in a line, she saw a row of support rods that held up the withered and long dead remains of a vine of some sort. Littering the ground, almost as if they had been discarded yesterday, were the tools of agriculture: a trowel, a bucket, some shears...the signs of a hard-fought life endured by those earliest of arrivals here on Harpers Reach.

Jez looked around. 'It's just like a museum.'

'Amazing isn't it? I guess it's exactly as it was the day the people who once lived here abandoned it.'

'You reckon that's what happened? They just upped and left all of a sudden?'

'Who knows? We've never found any skellys here. They just vanished.'

'Kinda spooky, huh?' replied Jez with a shudder.

Ellie noticed the gesture and laughed. 'You're not nervous are you?'

'No, of course not!'

A light gust of wind coursed through the greenhouse and towards an open hatch. It led back into the dark and grimy maze of the colony structure they had a few moments earlier emerged from. A gentle moan and the rattle of something loose deep inside disturbed the silence.

'It's just the wind,' Ellie said noticing Jez looking uncomfortably towards the entrance.

'Look, we can take the cat back home if you want. I can find my way in the dark.'

Jez frowned. 'No way! I'm not scared. Anyway,' she looked at the jimp sitting patiently at Ellie's feet, 'we've got Harvey to look after us.'

Ellie smiled through her mask. 'I love it here. I don't know why...I mean, it should be such a sad place. It's a community that failed somehow. I'd love to know what happened to the people here. Maybe they died, maybe they moved on. But, the thing is, they tried to build something with their own hands.'

Jez nodded, not really listening. She looked around. 'So we're going to camp out here?'

Ellie shrugged. 'If you think you're up for it, it's as good as anywhere. We can erect the oxygen tent in the middle of the greenhouse,' she said pulling her mask away from her face. She sampled the air. It wasn't rich enough to breathe for more than a minute or two without a supply of O2 to resort to. After half a dozen breaths, she started to feel light-headed and pulled the mask back down again over her mouth and nose.

The light was beginning to wane quickly as the bottom of the sun merged like molten liquid with the horizon.

'I should get the oxygen tent up whilst we still have some light,' said Ellie.

'I'm hungry. I'll go and get our supper,' said Jez.

Maria had made them some vegetable curry to take with them in a couple of thermos flasks, and a parcel of freshly baked bread to mop it up.

'Would it be quicker if I walked round the outside? Or go back through this spooky place?' asked Jez.

Ellie looked up and could see Jez was nodding reluctantly towards the open hatchway that led into the structure's gloomy interior. They had ambled their way through during the afternoon, casually exploring the dimly lit maze of carbon-fiber and metal corridors that linked one habitation module with the next. It had been lighter then of course, the sunlight streaming in through the many small windows and fractures in the walls and ceilings, casting dazzling shards of light diagonally across the murky confines around them, and lighting the dusty, grated floor in isolated pools. They had stopped frequently to bend down, pick up and study the faded, dust-coated signs of life scattered almost randomly across the various modules: combs, boots, cutlery, tools, ceramic-mugs...even a small plastic action figure - a solitary toy soldier patiently guarding this long abandoned outpost. These finds were everywhere, the debris, the *left-behinds* from two centuries ago, and as Jez and Ellie examined each one, the old place seemed to slowly come to life.

They had been wandering around for over two hours, meandering from one side of the colony to the other. Ellie guessed that the larger oxygen cylinders they had taken with them, were now about half empty. It would probably be a good idea if Jez made her way back through the structure to the cat and drove it around and parked outside the greenhouse. Then, it would be near to hand when they needed to replace the oxygen cylinders.

'It's much quicker going through...that is if you're okay going back on your own?'

Jez huffed indignantly, 'I'm not scared, if that's what you're suggesting. You want me to drive the cat round and park outside?'

'Yes, that's what I was thinking.' Ellie handed her a torch. 'Here, it's getting dark inside.'

Jez took the torch, flicked it on and panned it across at the dark void beyond the open hatchway. 'Okay then,' she muttered, licking her dry lips. 'Off I go.'

She stepped across the dry and crumbly ground. As she approached the entrance, she aimed the torch beam into the dark opening ahead of her and stepped inside. The sharp beam of torchlight picked out details on the corridor wall she hadn't noticed earlier in the afternoon as they had casually picked their way towards the greenhouse. Beside her she saw stenciled writing, faded by centuries of dry wind erosion; *connection conduit – locking this end only, exterior bulkhead, module section-NA156*. Nothing profound, just assembly instructions and registration numbers.

She ducked down to avoid tangling with a pipe and some wires that had spilled out of a panel in the ceiling above sometime in the distant past, and made her way forward through another bulkhead into a large habitation module beyond. It looked like it had been used for the storage of farming equipment and spare parts for machinery. As she made her way towards the conduit on the far side, she nudged another section of piping that hung down across the entrance and dislodged a cloud of dust and sand that sprayed across her face and hair.

'Aghh!!' she grunted, and spat several times. 'Lovely.'

*

Ellie fixed the oxygen tent with relative ease, a task she had carried out innumerable times before with the help of her Dad. When she had finished erecting the small two-person plastic cylinder, she attached a bottle of oxygen to the tent's inlet valve. The tent was big enough for her and Jez and Harvey to sleep in together. Jez was okay with sleeping head to toe with Ellie, but she had grumbled at the idea of sleeping so intimately with Harvey. But then, thinking about it, if Jez was bringing the cat round, then Harvey could sleep in the cabin instead if Jez really insisted.

Problem solved.

She finished her work on the tent in time to watch the very top of the sun flatten and slide along the horizon leaving a bloom of crimson light in the sky above.

'I love watching the sunset,' she said to Harvey. The jimp looked at her and cocked its head on one side.

'Sssssun-seeeettt?'

Ellie pointed towards the horizon, where the last light of day was rapidly diminishing. 'Over there, it's pretty isn't it?'

Harvey turned to look where she was pointing, and then looked back at her expressionlessly. He nodded. 'Like ssssun-seeeettt.'

He *likes* it? Ellie studied him curiously. 'You know Harvey, they say gene-imps aren't supposed to be able to like or dislike anything. That you don't have enough brain inside that thick skull to know what you *like*.'

Harvey tilted his head, and his brow furrowed with concentration. Maybe they were right. Harvey looked up at her and pointed one finger towards the sky.

'I like ssuunnnn-sssseet,' he said, and then pointed at her, 'I like Ehhh-leeeee.'

Ellie shook her head with amazement. 'There really is more to you than meets the eye, isn't there?'

She was positive she saw the faintest flicker of a smile on his lipless mouth.

CHAPTER 13

Jez spotted the shuttle a hundred yards away from where Ellie had parked the cat earlier that afternoon. From the black and white strip across the wings and the tail-fin, illuminated by landing lights, she could see it was a marshal's ship.

What's a city marshal doing out here?

Her first instinct had been to lay low inside the module she was in and see what was going on. She snapped off the torch and watched with growing curiosity through a scuffed, sand-blasted porthole as several torch beams flickered across the cat. She saw the silhouette of someone leaning forward to look inside the plexitex blister. The thought occurred to her that maybe something awful had happened to Ellie's family, or perhaps Aaron, and the police had arrived to bring the girls the news.

But then as the torch beams flickered around and across one of the men, she saw he was carrying a weapon.

That's not good.

She felt a cold thread of fear weave across her chest.

It was quiet out there, silent. The men - she counted six of them - began to move with a steady purpose towards the colony's buildings. She wondered how they could have arrived without either her or Ellie hearing the roar of the shuttle's engines. They must have cut them on approach and glided down stealthily. That was why it was parked so far away from the cat...to ensure even the un-powered *thud* of touchdown on the hard-baked clay wouldn't be heard.

As the dark forms drew nearer she could hear their voices. They spoke quietly and intermittently. Although she couldn't hear yet what they were saying, the intonation sounded foreign; they had off-world accents.

A torch beam flickered momentarily across the small porthole she was looking through and she quickly ducked out of sight, hoping that her sudden movement had not attracted any attention. Moments later she heard the rattle of footsteps up an entrance ramp and onto the metal grated floor, echoing down inside the colony structure towards her.

Freg, they're looking inside!

The footsteps grew louder and more numerous as it seemed all six shadowy figures had entered the interior. After a few moments they came to a halt. Jez guessed they were in the very next module to the one she was cowering in.

'So, they're in here somewhere,' said a voice muted by an oxygen mask, a softly spoken man. From the gentle tone of it, someone used to giving unquestioned orders. He didn't sound like a law marshal. 'Alright, let's not mess around here. Shoot them on sight, do you understand?'

She heard the murmur of assent from the others.

The softly spoken one continued more quietly. 'As soon as you've got their samples, Nathan....I want you to take them back, along with the Quin family tissue samples and prep them for testing. We'll take the first flight off this cruddy planet as soon as we're done here.'

The footsteps resumed again, growing louder as the men swept down the short connecting conduit towards her module.

Oh crud.

Jez scrambled across the floor and under a workbench as the dark module suddenly danced to life, illuminated by the beams of half a dozen flashlights as they panned from one side to the other.

'This place is a goddamned maze. We'll need to do this systematically. But before we go any further, you...'

'Yes, sir.'

'Disable the caterpillar. Without that they're not going to go anywhere.'

Jez heard one of the men leave the room, his echoing steps receding, and then there was silence, save for the distant moan of the wind and the mask-muffled draw and pull of several men breathing.

Jez struggled to sip the air from her mask as gently and quietly as she could.

*

Ellie heard the distant clatter of footsteps echoing all the way through the colony ruins to her. Harvey stirred uneasily and stared at the darkness beyond the open hatchway from which the noise had emerged.

'It's okay Harvey, just Jez tripping over her platform boots again, no doubt.'

There was nothing more to be heard except the fading echo. She wandered over towards the opening, pulled down her oxygen mask and cupped her hands.

'Jez!! You alright in there?'

*

Ellie's faint voice bounced down through the myriad of conduits and modules to where Jez hunched under the bench, and the men stood in silence only a few feet away from her.

'That's her! That must be the Quin girl,' said the softly spoken man.

'Which way did that come from?' one of the others said.

'I don't know. It could have come from any damned direction. We need to spread out and work our way across. You…'

'Yes, sir?' replied a gruff, deep voice. It sounded clipped and soldier-like.

'You stay here. When your colleague comes back, you can both follow us in. We're going to search every nook and cranny in this place, cabin by cabin. Nathan and you, take this exit. Leonard, you're with me, we'll take this one. Now let's go.'

Jez heard the rustling of movement and the clank of footsteps as the men filtered out of the module, leaving one of them behind; the one that sounded gruff like a trooper.

She waited as the footsteps of the other four receded, and then, cautiously leaning, she peeked around the edge of the workbench at the man waiting for his colleague to return from sabotaging the cat. By the light of his torch, which panned slowly around the enclosed space, she could make out very little, other than he was rather tall and carried a big gun.

A moment later she heard footsteps approaching.

'We've got to follow them in. We're searching this place from top to bottom.'

'Great,' said the other man with little enthusiasm. 'Starting in here?'

Jez hugged her knees tightly to her chest and gritted her teeth in anticipation. She saw the room dance again as the flashlights were cast haphazardly around.

'There's nowhere to hide in here.'

'What about behind that workbench?'

'Go look if you want, I'm catching up with the others. There's a bonus payment for the first shot on target. I'm not missing out on that.'

She heard one of the men head out of the room, walking swiftly. Then there was silence, save for the distant and echoing noises of the other men moving around the dark labyrinth dislodging dusty furniture, pulling open storage lockers, searching relentlessly for them.

Jez held her breath, afraid that the soft click of the oxygen valve in her mask would give her away. A long moment passed as the man in the same room as her deliberated whether this module was worth the trouble of searching, and then he stirred to life.

She saw the shadows in the room leap as the man's torch swung around towards one of the exits and he headed after his colleague.

Oh thank crud.

She listened as his footsteps receded and then her heart leapt once more as she heard, far too clearly, Ellie's echoing voice drifting through the winding corridors to her.

'Jez? What the hell is going on back there?'

*

Ellie stood in the entranceway panning her torch down inside the tunnel in front of her, Harvey standing beside, clutching her hand tightly, nervously. She could hear the bang and clatter of careless movement from inside. That was definitely the sound of *several* people moving around in there, she thought. There was somebody else in there, apart from Jez.

The noise of movement inside had instantly halted after she called out. Whoever it was had frozen in their activity. Whoever else was in there, they had heard her. And then she heard a voice, a man's voice, issuing an order loudly and clearly. The smooth carbon and metal walls carried his voice much further than he must have intended.

'The Quin girl is up ahead somewhere. Spread out and find her.'

Her stomach lurched uneasily and her heart suddenly began to pound. 'Oh my crud,' she whispered.

*

Dammit Ellie, don't call out again, please.

If she did, she was going to lead them right towards her. These men were going to find Ellie standing out in that greenhouse. They were going to find her, and kill her unless she found someplace to hide, and fast. Fearing that any second Ellie was about to call for her once more Jez sucked in several deep fluttering breaths, removed her mask and cupped her hands.

'ELLIE! HIDE! They're coming to get you!'

Her voice sounded deafening, ringing off the walls around her. Almost immediately she heard the scraping of feet and one of the men responding.

'That was just up here!'

Oh no!

She thought those two men had moved further inside the labyrinth, but they were only in the next module. She had only a second to react before they came back in and this time would probably make an effort to look beneath the work bench. She scrambled out from under it and raced across the small room for one of the two exits.

Halfway across, a torchlight flashed briefly over her body.

'Shit! Get her!'

The deafening metallic rattle of a pulse rifle filled Jez's ears, followed by the whistling, whining and rattle of slugs hitting the wall behind her and the metal floor at her feet.

She dived through the exit, leaving the module and staggering into the conduit beyond. She ran recklessly forward into complete darkness, her hands stretched out in front of her, groping blindly for any treacherous obstacles dangling from the ceiling ahead of her. The heels of her boots clattered and scraped against the metal floor, making enough noise that any blind man could find her.

*

Ellie heard the gunfire, and knew instantly what it was.
Hide! Hide! Hide!
She looked around the greenhouse. There was nowhere to hide out here, nowhere. She turned to look back into the dark corridor in front of her, towards the noises of hurried movement, exchanged whispered instructions, which were now growing louder as *they* were getting closer. She realized there was only one way to head, and leading Harvey by the hand, she ran back inside the dark warren, trying desperately to tread as lightly as she could. She fumbled her way down the conduit and into the first module; the farming tools and machinery storage room.

Ellie knew she had one advantage over whomever it was looking for her. She knew the layout reasonably well, having explored it thoroughly on many occasions before. Although whether she could find her way around in the dark, without any light at all, she was about to find out. She could only think of one good area in which to hide, the rest of the weather station was sparse enough that any cursory search would uncover her easily. The place she was thinking of offered her more of a chance to stay hidden for longer.

*

Jez tripped over a loose floor grating, stumbled and fell. As she pulled herself to her feet she turned to see over her shoulder the flickering light of an approaching torch. They were behind her, and closing the gap rapidly.

She snapped her torch on for a second, quickly studying the way ahead. She could see what looked like a place that had once been a communal area, a gathering space. Ellie had shown her round this 'hall' earlier this afternoon. They had wandered through it with shards of sunlight piercing through gaps in the failing ceiling, and dappling the dust-caked floor and over-turned plastic seats.

She struggled to remind herself where the exits were off this room, and where they led to, as she staggered forward into this larger module, the torch snapped off again before those behind her could see it. Almost immediately, her long legs tangled with several of those over-turned chairs scattered across the floor. The scrape and squeal of the chairs as they slid across the ground was horrifyingly loud. A moment later, she heard the men behind her calling out to their colleagues. 'There's one of them over here!'

Again, with no choice, she took a chance and snapped the torch on, panning it wildly around the room. To her left was an exit, to her right another one. She recalled from this afternoon's leisurely ramble that one of them led into a small storage room, once used as a pantry. The other led towards a maze of small, sleeping quarters…like mini habi-cubes of a sort. She could hide in the pantry, burrowing down behind racks that still contained sealed canisters of food that were probably still as fresh as the day they were sealed-in hundreds of years ago. But it was a dead-end. If they decided to search that, she would be trapped with no way out.

The cramped confines of the sleeping quarters offered her the best chance of staying hidden, cluttered as they were with all manner of personal lockers, trunks, bunkbeds and built in storage spaces. But she couldn't remember which of the two exits led that way.

Left or right? Come on Jez you butterhead. Which one?

She turned to the left, feeling her way cautiously with her hands, trying not to bump into and noisily disturb any more of the scattered bucket seats.

CHAPTER 14

Deacon ducked through the bulkhead and joined the two mercenaries standing in the short length of corridor, Leonard following behind him.

One of the mercenaries aimed his torch up the corridor, the light picking out what looked like a larger module beyond. 'We've got one of them up ahead there, sir,' he said.

'Who fired their weapon?' asked Deacon.

'It was me,' the same one answered.

'Did you hit her?'

'No, I don't think so.'

Deacon cursed silently. A trail of blood spots would have been useful. 'Alright, let's deal with this one first. Then we can flush out the other one at our leisure.'

He led them forward, lighting the way with his torch. He pulled out a hand gun from a holster strapped to his thigh. A slim, elegant gun, but powerful enough to knock anyone it hit off their feet.

This damned place was going to be a nightmare to track them down in, but then, there was nowhere to go. No one was leaving here. It was nicely isolated. This girl Ellie Quin would have been far wiser staying in New Haven, losing herself amidst the press of people there. She had played a good game up until now, staying one step ahead of him – fleeing her bolt hole in the city just in time, and then again driving out here, hoping to lose them in the wilderness. Her family had been dutifully tight-lipped about where she had headed...at first. But it was all over now, there was nowhere else for her to go, unless she fancied her chances running away on foot across the desert.

This could have been so much more difficult. If she had gone to ground in the city, flushing her out from New Haven's grubby streets would have required him to call in a great deal more manpower for the job. He might even have had to consider putting the whole damned city under quarantine to be safe; blocking all surface-to-orbit transit until this child was recovered. He had the authority to do that, of course. Hell, he had the authority, if it came to it, to have the whole damned planet sterilized with an orbital gamma pulse; make a clean sweep, leaving not a single soul alive. The stakes were *that* high. But then, he noted wryly, that several senior members of the

Committee had significant commercial interests on the planet, and would probably have castigated him for that, for overstepping his authority. Even though he might have saved them all from damnation by stopping the girl in time.

Deacon smiled in the darkness. The chase had gone well. Running her to ground *here* was as good as he could have hoped for. If the child and her friend wanted to play a little game of hide and seek, that was just fine. In fact, this was turning out to be a bit of fun.

He led them into the larger module and panned his torch around. It looked like some sort of communal hub for the colony, the equivalent of a town hall. He knew what these old colonial outposts were like, they followed a predictable pattern. A sense of community was everything to those early trailblazers. They bolted together their makeshift modular homes around the notion of a common room, a shared space where important decisions or disputes could be discussed or decided in a quaintly idealistic and democratic way. Every one of these tough old shanty towns had a space like this somewhere in the middle of it; a hub, with accommodation and utility wings branching out from it. He swung the torch beam across from one side to the other. Two exits as far as he could see.

He ordered two of the mercenaries to check the exit on the right first.

*

Jez could hear them turning over the storage room. They were getting frustrated and impatient by the sound of it. She puffed with relief that she chose the other exit and wasn't now trapped in that pantry with them.

She put her torch on, covering it with one hand so that most of the light was obscured. From the faint glow that emerged, she could see that she had remembered the layout of this place correctly. Up ahead, on either side of the corridor, were dozens of rounded doorways that each led directly into a domestic cubicle; simple, interconnected cubic living spaces each one designed for a couple or a small family. As she had discovered earlier - checking a few of them out with Ellie - many of them were furnished with basic cots and storage lockers, some still contained personal artifacts...poignant reminders that, once upon a time, not only hardy men and woman scratched a living here, but their children also.

She recalled there was one cubicle, approximately halfway along this long corridor on the right that had a particularly large storage trunk, tucked discreetly behind a rocking horse that had been crudely welded together long ago no doubt by some doting father from scraps of metal; a sad looking hand-made toy, with a multitude of rough edges, and sharp protrusions that must have chafed any poor child riding it.

She made her way as quietly as she could up the corridor, with her torch still on and covered by her fingers, listening carefully for the slightest sound of movement up ahead. She hoped to God Ellie had heard her warning cry and found somewhere to hide too. Ellie seemed to know this place like the back of her hand. Hopefully, she had found some little nook in which to lie low.

A noise up ahead.

Above the ever-present moan of wind, the slightest scrape of movement. Very close. She quickly snapped off her torch, pulled her oxygen mask away from her mouth and held her breath, waiting to see if another sound followed.

Clink.

A foot placed down just a little too heavily.

Shit-o-la.

Someone was up ahead at the other end of the corridor and moving down towards her. In the pitch black, Jez decided to feel her way forward to the next cubicle doorway, and if she could do it without noisily bumping into anything, she would silently slide into it, and let the party up ahead pass her by.

She crouched down and put one hand out in front of her face, feeling for any dangling nooses of wire, whilst her other hand fumbled ahead in the space in front of her feet for anything she might trip over. And, as quietly and quickly as she could, she scuttled forward.

She heard another footfall and then labored breathing; two masks clicking as the oxygen valves opened and closed. Whoever that was, they were very close.

Those sons-of-bitches had wised up and turned their flashlights *off* and were stalking her in the dark now. They probably even had night-vision goggles, similar to ones she had seen on a toob drama once; goggles that let you see anything in the dark, albeit with a spooky green tinge. One of *them* was probably already lining up a shot on her in the dark. She involuntarily cringed, her eyes clamped shut, her mouth hung open with a silent scream, dry as a desert, waiting for the inevitable echoing crack of gunfire.

Oh crud, get it over with you-

Her hand, stretched out in front of her and dug into something soft and wet.

'Ouch!' a voice yelped.

'Ellie?'

'Yes dammit! You just poked me in the eye,' she hissed angrily.

CHAPTER 15

Aaron checked his navigation display once more. He was nearly there. The floodlights of his shuttle lit the dark landscape below and ahead. He began to slow Lisa down. He would have thought by now that the glow of lights from the Quin farm would have been visible. It was late, but there would be some lights on, surely, somewhere. He scanned the horizon again, looking for the faint glow of some internal light even, diffused by the foggy transparency of a plastic dome.

Nothing.

He was almost upon the farm according to the navsat co-ordinates he had logged in after dropping the girls off. It had to be somewhere up ahead now.

All of a sudden, the brilliant glare of his floodlights was reflected back from something out there in the thick darkness of the night. A moment later the hemispherical outline of one of the smooth enviro-domes loomed into view.

There it is.

He slowed the shuttle down to a crawl, wary that the roar of his engines on full blast might wake up the whole family. He could settle her down gently on minimal power, not exactly a silent landing, but a little less of a disturbance. He circled the farm slowly, looking for a suitable place to set down. There was not a single light on anywhere, not even any faint night-lights in the central dome in which they lived.

He put the shuttle down in front of the entrance to one of the agri-domes and turned off his floodlights. As the dust settled he waited in his seat, the dim amber glow from the control panel the only source of illumination, allowing his eyes to adjust to the dark. He waited a few minutes to see if the dull rumble of his arrival had awoken anyone.

He had pre-arranged to come by and pick them up tomorrow morning some time. But the things he had needed to do in Harvest City had been accomplished with far less hassle than he had anticipated. And rather than accumulate another day's worth of docking fees, Aaron had decided to set off early, and a little presumptuously, park up overnight outside the Quin farm. He had even hoped he might be invited in for a little home cooking and in return, the following morning, he would happily offer to show Ellie's family around the shuttle in return. He knew she had a little brother who would no doubt go ape-wild over the experience.

But, no one seemed to have woken. He saw no lights coming on inside. And as he carefully studied the farm he noticed that the round hatch to the nearest agri-dome had been left wide open.

Hang on, that's not right.

Ellie's father was an oxygen farmer, leaving a door open like that would be a cardinal sin for him; a criminal waste of their yield. Aaron rose steadily from his seat and made his way towards the rear of the cabin, a growing sense of unease gnawing away at him as he grabbed a mask and prepared to exit.

*

It was unbearably hot and stuffy inside the storage locker. The three of them were squeezed together, an untidy tangle of limbs, most of them Harvey's. They breathed alternately with masks off and on, doing their best to extend the dwindling supply of oxygen in their masks' cylinders. There couldn't be much left, and soon they were going to have to do something, or they were going to suffocate.

Ellie took a guess that they had been in the locker now for over an hour. For the first twenty minutes or so, they had listened with a growing sense of panic as *they* moved tirelessly around from module to module, noisily, angrily hunting them down. Sometimes, judging from the noises, they seemed to be drawing closer, then for some reason heading away. Despite their best efforts, it didn't seem to be an organized or systematic search. They had checked some of the cubicles in the sleep quarters, but not all. At one point, they gave the cubicle next door to theirs the once over, pulling the sleeping cots loudly to one side and opening, and slamming shut, every cupboard and storage unit within.

Then, after a while, the noises had died down. The last sound of movement Ellie had heard had been - she guessed - about twenty minutes ago.

'We need to get some more oxygen,' she whispered to Jez.

'I know. I think mine's nearly out.'

Ellie pulled her mask down and took a few breaths. The air was poor, the O2 content low. She endured it as long as she could before starting to feel dizzy, then she pulled the mask up and sucked in another lungful of precious oxygen that restored her fogging mind.

'We need to get to the cat or the oxygen tent in the green house,' she whispered again.

'I know.'

'Soon.'

'Who are they?' asked Jez.

'I don't know...I just...'

'Is there anything you're not telling me?'

'Like what?' Ellie whispered. 'I...I've not done anything to anyone. I don't know why anyone would want me!' she added, a tone of desperation in her reply. 'Maybe they're criminals or terrorists or something...and this is their secret hide out.'

Jez had heard them use Ellie's name. They were after *her*. They sat in silence for a moment before Jez asked the question they were both thinking. 'Do you think they're gone?'

'I haven't heard them for a while now.'

Neither had Jez, but that meant nothing; they could be lying in wait. They certainly seemed ruthless and determined enough to sit tight until the job was done. She recalled the brief exchange she had heard when they had first entered the weather station, something about 'samples from the family'. Jez hadn't had time to dwell on what those few words actually meant, until now.

Oh, no. Please, not that. Not them.

If they got out of this mess alive, she wondered what appalling discovery might be awaiting poor Ellie. Jez had seen with her own eyes how close a family they were. Despite the fact that Ellie had run away from her life here, there was still a powerfully strong, almost magical, emotional bond between them all.

'What's that?' gasped Ellie.

It was something they both *felt* rather than heard; a deep vibration that caused the metal door of the storage locker to rattle ever so slightly.

'You think that was a shuttle engine?' whispered Jez hoarsely. 'They're going?'

'Sounded like it.'

The vibration increased in intensity for a few moments before beginning to diminish and finally, the gentle metallic tapping of the door against its frame ceased.

'Do you think it's safe to head out?' asked Jez.

'Give it a few minutes to be sure.'

*

Deacon watched their shuttle rise up a couple of hundred feet amidst a cloud of dust, then bank and head across the arid desert. He watched its navigation lights winking in the dark as they receded into the distance. Eventually, when the shuttle was far enough away that the orange and green wing-tip lights seemed to converge as one, he watched the ship set down on the ground again without a sound, several miles away.

The ruse would surely flush these girls out.

It had become patently obvious that he didn't have enough men to search the abandoned installation thoroughly, there was too much of it, and clearly these two girls had a good knowledge of the layout. They could spend endless hours going in circles, searching one area then the next, only to find those two had discreetly scuttled past them from one bolt-hole to another.

If they packed up and left now, the two girls would die when the last of their air was spent. But Deacon needed bodies. He needed a sample to be sure Ellie Quin was Mason's handiwork.

No, the shrewd way to play this was to sit tight and wait for them to come out. Unless they had managed to secure an additional supply of oxygen, they would surely be running out of whatever they had on them at the point they went to ground. His men had found the oxygen tent set up in what looked like the colony's old greenhouse, and there was also additional oxygen inside the caterpillar, parked outside the entrance. At some point they would have to make a dash for one of those, or suffocate somewhere in the ruins.

He had sent two of the mercenaries and the lab technician, Nathan, to hunker down in the module nearest the front entrance. It overlooked the caterpillar. They were now hiding in the dark and keeping an eye on the vehicle whilst he, Leonard and the third mercenary were lying low in the shadows of the greenhouse and watching the tent.

They had been quietly holding these positions now for twenty minutes. He had instructed the shuttle to wait a while before lifting off and ostensibly leaving the scene, so that the combined period of quiet followed by the noise of it taking off would hopefully be enough to convince them that the coast was finally clear.

Even if they were still suspicious, they needed that oxygen. Deacon looked at the faint glow of the holo display on his watch. They *had* to be out of air by now, or very close to it.

CHAPTER 16

Ellie's mask was faltering. The last breath she had taken from it had delivered a less than adequate hit of oxygen. The supply in the attached cylinder was all but gone, a few more minutes at best, and then she would be going on whatever traces of oxygen her lungs could filter from the air in and around the ruins.

'I'm out, how're you doing?' she asked Jez.

'Me too I think.'

Ellie looked down at Harvey who, it seemed, had been drawing less oxygen from his mask than either of them. He looked okay for now though they might have to share the oxygen left in his mask if it came to it.

'Then we have to go, or die here,' replied Ellie, a shudder of trepidation catching her muted voice.

'Yeah, we've got no choice,' Jez reluctantly agreed.

With a gentle creak, they pushed the door to the storage locker open. Jez turned on the torch and quickly panned it around. 'It looks clear,' she whispered.

They climbed out and Ellie led the way to the cubicle's doorway. She waited until Jez and Harvey had stopped moving and listened intently for a few moments. There was only silence.

She reached out for the jimp, felt his coarse skin and quickly found one of his hands. 'The quickest way out is left, through the community hall, take a right and head for the entrance module,' she whispered quietly.

'Got it,' replied Jez.

'Then let's go.'

With only the faintest glow leaking from the end of the finger-smothered torch, they padded down the corridor towards the large communal module. The hatch had been left open by one of the men who had trawled down this way earlier. As they drew closer, by the faint glow of the torch, they could see from the disturbed centuries-old layer of clay dust, the footprints, the scrape marks, that the room had been thoroughly searched.

They entered it warily. Jez briefly uncovered the torch and panned it around the hall, before covering it once more.

'Looks clear,' she hissed.

Ellie led Harvey by the hand across the space, sticking close to the wall to avoid knocking into any of the chairs and benches scattered haphazardly across the floor. They reached the bulkhead leading to the passageway beyond. The hatch had been left firmly shut.

The last of the oxygen in Ellie's mask was gone, the valve clicking yet not giving her any more. She pulled it off her face, and dropped it. 'No good now,' she whispered, beginning to gasp from the paucity of O_2 in the air around her.

Harvey instinctively understood and pulled the mask from his face. 'Eh-leeee,' he said softly, offering it to her. She reached for the mask, pulled it over her mouth and took several deep breaths before passing it back to him.

Jez removed her mask. 'Crud, mine's just gone too.' She casually pulled the mask away from Harvey's face and placed it over her mouth, and sucked in three or four breaths before letting him have it back.

'Thanks Harv,' she said, patting his head like a dog.

Ellie grabbed hold of the hatch and pulled it open. It creaked and clicked as the ancient hinge complained; the noise echoed worryingly down the corridor beyond. It wasn't too far now. Just twenty feet or so along this section, through into a small module, another short passageway and then the cabin that functioned as the foyer entrance for the colony.

Ellie, still holding in her lungs the last breath she had sucked in from Harvey's mask, led the way into the corridor. Their pace was faster this time. The necessity to find oxygen was the increasingly urgent driving factor now. They passed down the length of the corridor quickly and stepped into the small module beyond, little more than a small round, widened section where a number of pipes and cable junctions converged at a maintenance point. With a final shared glance of hope, Jez nodded and they both advanced side by side, each leading Harvey by one of his hands, down the short and final length of corridor towards the entrance module.

A blinding flashlight snapped on ahead of them.

There was no verbal warning issued for them to stop, just the click of a weapon's safety being flicked off and the deafening burst of a short volley, accompanied by the dazzling flash of strobing light coming from the pulse rifle.

Ellie felt a warm pulse beside her left ear and a streak of white-hot agony along the right side of her neck. She dropped to her knees clutching at her throat. Jez dropped to the floor beside her.

Harvey's head spun both left and right to see both of his owners on the ground beside him. His soft voice was at first a low keening which quickly changed to an enraged howl that startled Ellie, as she slumped to a sitting position, still clutching her bloody throat and gasping for air.

Jez looked up in surprise as the jimp hurled himself forward, propelled powerfully by his short legs, towards the torchlight. A second later, the torch was knocked aside, and in the flickering light as the hand that held it thrashed around wildly, they saw the four powerful arms of their jimp flail with brutal intent at the man that he had latched himself onto.

'Get this thing off me-e-e-e!!!!!!' a man's voice screamed desperately. The wretched cry ended with a gurgle.

Jez impulsively pushed herself to her feet and ran forward, her torch now no longer covered by her fingers, revealing the chaos ahead more fully. Dark strips of liquid splashed across the small room as Harvey, a whirling blur of grey motion, ferociously beat at the unfortunate man's head and chest.

A second man stood beside them, fumbling with an ammo clip dislodged by a blow from one of Harvey's flailing arms. Jez, taking advantage of the momentary confusion, and emboldened by Harvey's unpredictable full-frontal assault, charged towards him. The man managed to slam the clip in, hip-aim the gun towards the jimp and fire a sustained burst at the rippling grey body.

Harvey was hurled by the impact of a dozen bullets against the metal wall beside the exit, his dark blood sprayed in viscous stripes across it.

Jez swung the two foot length of the torch horizontally across the man's face as he turned towards her, his gun swinging round to deal with the new threat. The heavy, bulb-end of her torch caught his chin with a sickening crunch, and his head and body spun like a top as he flopped unconscious to the ground. Jez collapsed on top of him.

And then there was a moment of calm.

Jez, gasping from the exertion and the lack of good air, turned back round to look at Ellie, who was beginning to scramble to her feet. 'Ellie!!' she screamed, seeing a torrent of blood streaming over the hand pressed into her neck, and down her front.

'I'm okay. I think it just snicked me,' Ellie replied shakily, struggling for breath like Jez. 'Oh my crud, they got Harvey,' she added stooping down to place a hand on his narrow chest, torn open by half a dozen ragged holes.

Harvey stirred, his all-black eyes opened and focused on Ellie leaning over him.

'Harvey,' Ellie whispered, tears already welling up in her eyes. 'You're going to be alright,' she said soothingly, stroking his cheek.

'Harv-eeeee, good?'

She smiled and nodded. 'You were very good. You saved me and Jez.'

Harvey reached up with one of his arms and a finger gently brushed her eyes. The jimp curiously inspected the drop of moisture on the tip of his finger.

'Whattt isssss?'

Ellie swallowed hard. 'It's a tear. It means I'm sad, Harvey.'

Harvey nodded, understanding. 'I ssssaaadd tooo.' The jimp exhaled a final gurgling breath and then sagged, his sightless eyes staring down the passageway.

'Oh Jez,' she gasped. 'Why are they doing this to us?'

'You two better run now,' said someone from a dark corner of the room.

Jez spun round and aimed the torch towards where the voice seemed to have come from. Another man was kneeling in the corner, his pulse rifle aimed squarely at Jez. 'Which one of you is Ellie Quin?'

Ellie found herself raising a hand like a child in a classroom. 'Me,' she replied weakly.

The man studied her for a moment. 'Your wound looks minor. You'll live.'

'You're not g-going...going to kill us?' she asked.

'No. But you must leave now,' he answered gruffly, 'before the others arrive.'

Jez was now struggling unbearably for breath and sagged to her knees.

The man hesitated for a moment before lowering his gun and pulling out an oxygen mask from a survival pack slung low on his hip. 'Here take it,' he said, tossing it across to her, 'share it with your friend, but get out of here now. You've got seconds before the others get here!'

Jez grasped the mask, pulled it over her mouth and took half a dozen reviving mouthfuls of air, before handing it to Ellie who did the same. In the distance, they could hear the pounding of feet along the metal grating of a distant corridor.

'Go! The others are coming,' he said again, looking anxiously down the corridor.

'Why are people after me?' asked Ellie through the mask.

'Don't know. I'm just a hired hand. I was hired to kill you, but someone else has paid me twice what these people did to help you get away. I don't know why, I don't care why. Now just-'

'But why does-?'

'There's no time for any of this!' the man growled quietly. 'If you don't go now, I'll have to kill you myself. Otherwise *they*,' he nodded towards the approaching sound of footsteps, 'will know I'm getting a payment from somewhere else. That's a death sentence for me. So you better move now, or *I will* kill you!' he said readying his gun.

Ellie reached out with one hand and grabbed Jez's. 'The cat, Jez...let's go!'

Jez scrambled to her feet and the two girls turned and fled outside into the night. Ellie staggered across the uneven ground towards the caterpillar. It was a slow vehicle, but faster than a person could run. If they could start the thing up in time and get going before those other men arrived...

'Ellie! Look!' shouted Jez, pointing up into the sky.

Ellie followed the direction she was pointing and saw a shuttle coming in towards them low and fast, two brilliant beams of light sweeping the ground ahead of it.

'It's Aaron I think!' she screamed.

Both girls waved their arms frantically in the air as they continued to run from the entrance of the weather station. One of the floodlights swung across Ellie and steadied on her.

'Please Aaron!' she yelled, 'quickly!!!'

They heard a burst of gunfire. Jez turned to see the man who had let them go, standing outside the entrance running down the ramp, firing his weapon towards them, but intentionally, marginally, wide of them. A moment later he was joined outside by three other men. All three aimed with far greater accuracy and divots of orange clay and dust jumped from the ground into the air either side of their feet, as both girls continued to run desperately out into the desert towards the approaching shuttle.

The shuttle descended quickly, the access ramp at the back of the hold already beginning to open and extend for them with the high-pitched whine of servo-motors audible above the deafening, deep rumble of the landing thrusters as they kicked in.

Another rattle of gunfire, and Jez felt the hot buzz of a shot whistle through her hair and past her cheek.

'oh freg-freg-freg-freg,' she muttered as she raced towards the ramp, now twelve feet, now ten feet above the ground, as Aaron brought the shuttle down.

Ellie hurled herself onto the ramp as it thumped heavily against the ground, and Jez landed with thud beside her a second later.

'Come on take her up, you big lump!' Jez shouted, knowing full well that Aaron wouldn't be able to hear her. The shuttle remained on the ground, the thrusters still roaring at a constant pitch, blasting the ground viciously, the air filling with a dense cloud of dust.

The men outside the entrance to the weather station were now running towards them, weapons firing. The ramp rattled and sparked with the impact of shots slamming home around them

'Come on!!!!!' Ellie screamed.

'Go-go-go-go-go!!!!!' Jez bellowed hoarsely.

The pitch of the thrusters dropped momentarily and for one terrifying moment Ellie thought Aaron was winding them down. But then with a burst of renewed power, and an alarming jolt that nearly shook Ellie off the ramp, the shuttle began to lift off again, and the ramp began to rise.

Ellie and Jez began to pull themselves up the ramp, clawing at the corrugated grooves in the metal to stop from sliding off the rising access ramp and down into the swirling sandstorm beneath them.

An elbow appeared over the lip of the ramp and then a head appeared as one of the men desperately pulled himself up after them. Ellie looked down at him and recognized the face as the mercenary who had just let them go. He shouted something urgently at Ellie which she failed to hear over the roar of the thrusters and the continued rattle of gunfire from below.

But she guessed what he was asking her to do, and obligingly she kicked out at his face so that he dropped back down to earth before the height was enough that the fall would kill him. With the servo-motors whining against the load, the ramp continued to rise upwards until angled at forty-five degrees, and nearly closed, Ellie and Jez rolled down it and tumbled into the passengers' suite, one on top of the other.

With a final grinding thud, and the lock of restraining bolts, the ramp sealed the hold and shut off the roar of noise outside.

*

Deacon watched the shuttle bank steeply and pull up and away from them into the purple sky above. In the distance, several miles away, he could see the police shuttle finally, belatedly, rising up off the ground, but the response had been too damned slow. And anyway, it was an old vessel, even older than this big, white-painted mongrel of a vessel that was fast fading into the night. They would never be able to catch up with it.

He'd nearly had her. So bloody nearly.

He'd had Mason's little monster in the palm of his hand, and she'd managed to escape him again.

'Fuck it!!!' he snarled to himself.

His first instinct was to howl with rage and lash out furiously at someone. But composure was everything to him. Cursing, spitting venom at some subordinate, stamping his feet with frustration wasn't going to get him anywhere. That sort of behavior was for someone who lacked control, discipline; someone who was losing it.

And he was so very far from losing it.

In fact, there was a very thick silver lining here to hold onto whilst he calmed himself, steadied his heartbeat, his pulse, his mind.

Ellie Quin is most definitely Mason's candidate. She was smart. Wily. And very fast. Exactly how he'd engineer such an abomination. But that was something he could confirm soon enough. There was a lot of blood in that entrance module, the girl was wounded, some of that had to be hers. He had a sample now.

Look on the bright side...

He now had a name, images and data on her, gleaned from the census and immigration databases here on Harpers Reach. The alternative was that he could still be pointlessly trawling through names on a list back at the labs orbiting Pacifica. He could so easily have picked the *wrong* planet to begin narrowing down his search.

Deacon smiled calmly. He had the right child and now there was nowhere she could hide on this planet. And more importantly, there was no way she was going to find a way off-world either.

Enough is enough.

Discretion be damned, this whole godforsaken backwater mud-ball was going to be quarantined immediately. Enough messing around; he would contact the Administration immediately and have the nearest military ships diverted this way to fully enforce the quarantine. A cover story could be worried about later on; an outbreak of something horrible and airborne. The most important thing right now was to make sure this little girl didn't make it off-world.

CHAPTER 17

We have pinpointed the planet on which Mason's child is located.

Have you found the child?

We have an identity, and we are closing in on it.

Are you satisfied that you will locate it?

There is a risk the child might find a way off-world. She has friends helping her. Under the authority you have given me I will place the planet under quarantine.

Which planet?

Harpers Reach.

There are commercial interests there for members of the committee. Are you certain this is necessary?

It is a necessary precaution.

We will issue a universal announcement that a dangerous and infectious pathogen has taken hold there. You will also have whatever military vessels can be spared to deploy as you wish.

Thank you. I have a concern you should be made aware of.

Proceed.

I suspect that the child is being assisted covertly. Although she may not be aware of what she is, it seems she is aware that we are after her. I suspect she has been warned by someone with access to information.

A traitor?

It may be that Mason was not acting alone, that the conspiracy is more widespread.

Within the committee?

That is a possibility to consider.

We shall be cautious. For now, you must continue to operate on your own authority, do whatever you deem necessary and catch this child before it is too late.

I understand.

CHAPTER 18

Jez squeezed through the gap between the arm rests and settled down in the co-pilot's seat. 'She's asleep.'

Aaron set the autopilot on and turned to her. 'How is that wound?'

'I don't know. I've seen enough episodes of Dr Emergency to guess it looks worse than it is. The bleeding has stopped anyway and I splashed on some Anti-Bact and put a bandage on it. I'm more worried about how much toxic crud both Ellie and I breathed in out there.'

'You'll be alright,' replied Aaron, 'you might have a doozy of a migraine for a few days though.'

They sat in silence for a moment, accompanied by the muted, deep bass rumble of Lisa's engines as she sped low across the desert.

'So where are you taking us?'

'To Harvest City. Things are much less organized over there, it's easier to stay anonymous.'

Jez looked up at him. 'I don't know what's going on Aaron, but somebody really wants our Ellie dead.'

Aaron nodded. 'You mustn't tell her this now, Jez….not until she's ready for it, but…'

'But what?'

'I found her family.'

Jez turned to look at him, the question forming on her lips, but he nodded before she could ask.

'Oh no.' Jez felt like she had been punched in the chest. A horrible suspicion was all she'd had. She gasped. 'I heard them say things about them, I wasn't sure what they meant. Oh crud, oh God...poor Ellie. They're all…?' Jez couldn't bring herself to say the word.

Aaron remained silent for a moment, frowning as he tried to erase the appalling images from his mind. He had found the father slumped defensively over the children, a testament to his final act as the shots were fired. The mother had been worked on afterwards – presumably to find out where Ellie was, and left for dead. Their home ransacked, gutted - Ellie's entire childhood world casually destroyed and ripped to shreds.

'Not all of them, not when I arrived,' Aaron's voice faltered. 'Her mother was still alive. She told me where to find you, before she...' he turned to look out of the window, quiet for a moment. 'Look, let's just keep that our secret for now.'

Jez nodded silently. 'Oh god, poor Ellie,' she muttered quietly.

'You know her better than I do,' said Aaron, 'do you have any idea why people are after her?'

She shook her head. 'No. She's just another farm girl. She's never told me anything that, that made her....*different* I guess. She's a little dreamier than most, quiet, focused, but you know all this anyway, right? Ellie herself hasn't got a clue why they're after her.'

Aaron turned round in his seat to check she was still sleeping.

'She's just a regular girl,' Jez continued, 'and the closest thing *I've* ever had to family, I guess.'

'Did you hear *anything* from those men that might help us know who's after her?'

Jez shook her head. 'Just bits and pieces that don't make sense.' She stopped and her eyes widened. 'One of the men let us go. He said he'd been hired to go after Ellie, but also hired by someone else to see she got away.'

'You mean there are *two* groups of people interested in her?'

Jez shrugged, 'I guess so.'

Aaron shook his head. A few hours ago, if he'd been asked if there was anything about his young friend Ellie Quin that he would consider unusual, he would have said she was a little more introspective than most, perhaps a little smarter than most people her age…but now? He racked his mind for anything she might have said or done that would explain why someone out there desperately needed her dead.

'I think they might be terrorists of some kind,' said Jez.

'Why?'

Jez considered the answer for a full minute. 'Well who else can you think of?'

'The authorities maybe, the Administration?'

Jez scoffed at the answer. 'What? The Administration??? Come on Aaron, they don't go around murdering people like that.'

'How do you know?'

'What?' Jez spun in her chair towards him. 'You're kidding, right? They hold the whole universe together. If it wasn't for them running things, making sure there's peace everywhere, we'd all be clubbing each other with sticks and stones. I know *some* history Aaron, I'm not entirely stupid. I've watched some documentaries. And you know, there are a few groups out there, groups of sicko terrorists that do stuff like that - grab people as hostages and do really nasty things to them...kill children, kill women. They don't like the fact that everything's just fine, that there aren't any wars to fight. *They* hate that.'

Jez shook her head with disbelief at him. '*They* are the scumbags the Administration protects us from, Aaron. *Terrorists*. Maybe some of those sick drekks have found their way onto Harpers Reach, trying to turn our world into a screwed-up psycho-mess, just like the twisted screwed-up worlds they come from.'

'Terrorists?' He shook his head. 'You are so naive for someone street-smart.'

'Well, come on, it certainly isn't the Administration. I mean why would they fregging well do it? What harm was Ellie's family doing to them?'

Aaron shrugged. 'I don't know. But then why would terrorists kill them?'

Jez shook her head. 'We should go to the nearest law marshal and-'

Aaron cut her off. 'Jez...they arrived in a New Haven Authority vessel, a law marshal shuttle. I saw it on the ground on my approach in. We can't go to the police.'

Jez looked at him. She saw that too. 'So, maybe it was stolen?'

'Possibly. But look, I think that until we know who we're dealing with, we must keep to ourselves.'

Jez studied him in silence.

'I can't understand what the Administration would want with Ellie either,' Aaron continued, 'but the law marshals here on this planet can be bought by anyone Jez...*anyone*. They're just goons in uniform. Come on, you're a city girl, you know that as much as I do, surely.'

Jez bit her lip and nodded slightly. 'So what are we going to do?'

'I don't know. They'll be looking for her and they'll be looking for this shuttle. If I had the money I'd pay for us all to get a ticket off-world on the next ship going. But I don't. The best I can suggest is that we head for Harvest City, we stock up on fuel and supplies, and then we lose ourselves somewhere remote on this planet, and we lie low for a while.'

'What if you *sold* the shuttle?'

'Hell, we'd have enough money to buy ourselves out of this system and the next, but *they,* whoever *they* are, Jez, would track the sale down in the blink of an eye. You can't sell a vehicle like this without cutting a lot of red tape and a lot of data changing hands. And if *they* can secure the use of an authority vessel, they can sure as hell have access to vessel purchase and sale records.'

Jez looked out of the window. 'I'm scared Aaron…and I don't normally scare that easily,' she said, a solitary tear rolling down her cheek. 'We're in a real fregging mess.'

Aaron reached out grabbed her arm firmly. 'This isn't the best time to go crumple up, Jez. What you need to do is be strong, for Ellie's sake. She needs us both now.'

Jez looked down at his grasping hand. Any other man, any other time…and Jez would have balled-up her fist and slammed it into something soft and sensitive. But Aaron was the only friend she and Ellie had, and right now he was making a lot of sense, while, on the other hand, she was starting to gibber like some weak-kneed little waif.

'Yes, you're right,' she replied wiping the tear away and thumping her thigh with a fist for allowing herself to look so pathetic in front of him.

'So, we have a plan then,' he said. 'We'll land in Harvest City's port, stock up as quickly as we can, and then we go and hide out in the wilderness for a while.'

'And no mention of Ellie's family,' she added.

He nodded, 'not for now. Not for a while.'

*

The following day, Ellie watched the approach and descent with Jez, standing behind Aaron's seat, resting her elbows on the cushioned headrest. She squinted as the late afternoon sun bathed the cockpit with a brilliant sepia glow, and the windshield glared and shimmered.

Harvest City was a far less inspiring sight on approach than New Haven. Instead of one giant enviro-dome encasing the entire urban jungle, Harvest City was built from several hundred much smaller domes, each linked together by tubular throughways on the ground and, in some cases, several hundred feet up. It was a chaotic and modular structure, rather than a grand, imposing one. It was a city that had clearly built itself up organically over a long period, one dome at a time.

The port bore no resemblance whatsoever to that of New Haven's. Instead of a thousand-acre, checker-board landing field of color-coded pads, Ellie could see about a hundred or so hangars of varying sizes arranged either side of a long sealed concourse that led across the arid landscape towards the bubble-wrap carpet of Harvest City.

Aaron hovered several hundred feet in the air until he received a data handshake and a green guidance light began to blink above one of the smaller hangers. The shuttle, under the remote control of the port's automated landing guidance system, steadily dropped in altitude until it hovered outside the entrance to the hangar. Then, with a gentle nudge from the aft thrusters, it drifted forward, out of the brilliant glare of sunlight and into the gloomy, pale blue strip lighting within. A moment later, the shuttle settled onto the ground with a soft bump.

'So here we are,' said Aaron, looking around the small hangar anxiously for anything that might indicate some kind of reception party. 'It doesn't look like anyone's expecting us,' he added with a tone of relief.

'Let's hope,' added Ellie, absentmindedly rubbing the dressing on her neck. It throbbed painfully whenever she turned her head in either direction.

'Alright then, let's not push our luck. We need food supplies and fuel and we need to arrange that as quickly as we can.'

'Ellie and I can go and get the food,' Jez volunteered. She wanted to keep her friend as busy as possible. Ellie had been very quite over the last two days, brooding over Harvey, and clearly worrying about what lay ahead for them.

'Good. You'll find supply vendors all along the concourse, just outside the hangar. Buy as much as you can carry,' Aaron said holding out a wad of notes.

'Oh-my-god, is that actually *paper* money?'

'Yes. We shouldn't use cred-cards. It's traceable.'

'People here *use paper money?*' Jez was staring at the roll of notes as if it was an ancient Egyptian scroll of papyrus.

'Jesus, yes! Okay? Take it!' He handed the roll of notes over. 'While you're doing that, I'll arrange to have the ship refueled.'

Both girls left the shuttle and headed across the hangar floor towards a bay door signed 'exit to concourse', while Aaron strode purposefully over to a waiting maintenance technician to make arrangements for the swiftest turnaround that a bribe could buy.

As they approached, the hangar door slid open revealing a busy scene beyond; a bustling marketplace full of traders and shuttle owners and passengers pushing trolleys full of supplies before them.

Ellie found herself feeling a little more comfortable amid the swirling, noisy mass of people in the concourse - a fifty foot wide, windowless tunnel that stretched in both directions as far as she could see. Surely nothing was going to happen to them with so many people around.

'So, Ellie, what should we buy?' asked Jez.

Ellie shook her head distractedly. 'I don't know.'

'A load of protein paste I guess, and some synthi-caff for Aaron...we know he needs that or he gets all cranky. And I need some little luxuries too, or I'll just die,' Jez replied with a forced smile. She looked at Ellie, and then cupped her chin. 'Hey Ellie, we're all in this together,' she added, 'I need you just as much as you need me, eh?'

Jez was right. There were things that needed doing, and quickly. She spotted a discarded trolley and quickly walked over and grabbed it before anyone else could lay claim to it. 'Give me half the paper money. I'll go and get the paste, if you want to get the other things. It'll speed things up,' said Ellie.

Jez smiled. 'Good idea. Let's meet back here,' she turned round to look at the door that had closed behind them. 'Our hangar is 47, meet you here in twenty minutes, okay?'

Ellie watched Jez push her way forcefully through the crowd, the bright colors of New Haven fashion contrasting noticeably with the duller-hued, more practical garments of the people swirling around her. Ellie looked down at her own clothes; the bright green polylatex boots, her orange pants, and the blue smock were somewhat less flamboyant than Jez's outfit, but still she stood out just as much from the travelers and tradesmen all around her.

No time to worry about that now.

No, there wasn't. They needed to get these supplies and head back out into the wilderness as quickly as possible. Ellie pushed her cart forward as she scanned the signs above the various stalls lining each side of the concourse. At the same time her eyes darted nervously from one person to the next, looking anxiously for anyone studying her too intently.

Amid the push of people, her hand reflexively reached out for Harvey's...only to remember with a stab of pain, that he was gone. She realized that after their scramble to escape from the weather station, and the day and night aboard the shuttle hurtling with all speed towards Harvest City, all the time worrying and fretting over these mysterious people that wanted her dead, she hadn't spared much thought for the poor creature. Harvey's unexpected and savage attack on those men had actually scared her a little. She knew the jimp had attached himself to her, perhaps even felt something like affection for her...but she never in a million years would have predicted that he would hurl himself so ferociously onto another human to protect her like he had. A demonstration of naked aggression like that was supposed to be impossible for a jimp to carry out; according to the manufacturers, that is. Harvey had undoubtedly saved her and Jez, but she wondered whether she would ever feel totally comfortable alone with a gene-imp again, particularly one engineered for manual labor. She nervously recalled those powerful, muscular arms wrapped around Ted as he'd play-wrestled with the jimp, and shuddered to think what might have happened to her little brother if he had somehow convinced Harvey that he was a threat to her.

Just goes to show...you never know. All the same, she was going to miss the little creature. That brave little creature.

Poor Harvey.

She spotted a food supplies vendor, and pushed the trolley across the concourse towards the stall.

CHAPTER 19

He spotted her almost immediately as she, and her tall friend, emerged from the hangar. Amongst the thick crowd of shuttle delivery men, and farmers and outbackers in for the day to pick up essentials, they stood out.

They stood out way too much. Dangerously so.

He watched them discreetly from across the concourse as they discussed what to do. It was pathetically obvious what their plan was; to replenish their supplies and then go out into the bland wilderness of this planet and what? Hope things would blow over?

Things had suddenly become very dangerous. Somehow the Administration had caught wind of his plan, and they had released their hunting dogs after her scent. They weren't going to rest until she was dead, and her corpse sealed up and returned to their labs to study.

How the hell did they manage to track her down so damned quickly?

Millions of Paternity Requests, *millions* of them. Millions of mid-term fetuses shipped to planets throughout Human Space. How did they pick out the right child so damned fucking quickly? How did they manage that?

Mason cursed under his breath. The fact was they were onto her already. Unless she found a way off the planet immediately they were going to acquire her very quickly, and many, many years of preparation, a lifetime's work, would be wasted.

He watched the two girls split up, the taller one heading further down the concourse leaving Ellie Quin on her own.

Good. The tall one with her bright look-at-me clothes was like a damned beacon, begging for attention. He followed Ellie as she moved slowly through the crowd, her mind it seemed, a trillion miles away. She needed to be more alert, paying attention to her surroundings.

Ellie Quin, you need to be much, much sharper than this.

Now that the Administration seemed to be aware of his plan, everything was different. All bets were off. Mason knew he needed to act quickly to get her as far away as possible. The Administration were most probably already preparing to lock down the entire planet. That's how they worked. Not subtly, not when they needed to fix something. Their efforts would be overt, excessive with scant regards for lives lost. The disinformation would all come later; blaming any body count, any explosions, or a massacre of innocent bystanders on some separatist group or anti-administration terrorists.

And Ellie - the poor girl was so unprepared for this. There should have been a lot more time for her to mature, to ready herself, with him watching over her development, perhaps even directly mentoring her. But they had taken him by surprise, arriving out of nowhere, descending on Harpers Reach and zeroing in on her so terrifyingly quickly. Time had suddenly run out for her, for him, and she was going to need all the help she could get to stay ahead of them now.

He watched her barter for some food supplies; sacks of that appalling protein sludge that most people on this world seemed to eat routinely. And then she checked the time.

Yes, girl...time is running out for you. Tick-Tock, Tick-Tock.

There wasn't much of it left; the hunting dogs were bound to be here in this city already and quite probably had already detected her scent.

*

Ellie looked at the trolley. She had bought as many sacks of the paste as she had money for. Eight heavy sacks of the stuff. Each one would probably do her, Jez and Aaron two weeks. She decided to return to hangar 47, it was two hundred yards back up the concourse. The sooner she and Jez were back in the hangar and aboard the shuttle and ready to go, the better.

She pulled the trolley round and steered to one side of the central throng of people, hugging the wall behind the stalls out of the main flow of ambling foot traffic, doing her best to make her way back unnoticed, unseen.

As she passed behind a long stall, its large back wall shadowing the narrow walk space behind it, she felt a hand on her arm. She spun round, her mouth agape, one hand raised and ready to lash out.

An old man stood before her, the face vaguely familiar.

'Ellie, if you want to live, listen to me now,' he said quietly.

'Wh-who are you?' she muttered nervously, her heart pounding almost as much now as it had done amongst the ruins of the weather station.

'It doesn't matter who I am. Who *you* are, is far more important.'

'What? Why?'

'I don't have time for that now. Listen to me very carefully. I've arranged a way off of this world for you.'

'Huh?'

'Harpers Reach is about to be closed down, quarantined. Right now there are military ships heading this way and within hours, sometime this afternoon, maybe even sooner, the planet will be thoroughly blockaded. Nothing will be allowed down to the surface, nor up into orbit,' said the old man hurriedly. 'And this is all because of *you*.'

'Oh my crud,' Ellie whispered breathlessly. 'What have I done?'

'Just listen. A surface-to-orbit barge is waiting for you in hangar 113. I paid an enormous sum for them to accept you and one other as *un-credited cargo*. But they won't wait for long. I've warned them about the impending quarantine and the owners are understandably anxious for their barge to leave as soon as it can.'

With that, the old man checked the time. 'You have just over forty minutes left until they go without you. And they will, Ellie, if you're not there on time.'

Ellie stared at him, the face was so familiar. She had seen it within the last week, perhaps two. 'Who are you?'

'Wrong question, Ellie,' he replied. 'You should be asking, who are *you*?'

'I don't understand.'

'You are special. I made you what you are.'

Ellie frowned, confused.

'You are so important. And you need to understand why. Here-,' Mason handed her a small data disc. 'When you have time, play it. But not right now. Now you must decide which of your two friends you will take with you.'

Ellie shook her head, confused, beginning to feel a growing surge of panic. 'I'm not leaving either of-'

'Good God!' the old man hissed angrily. 'You need to start being smarter than this, girl. Think!!! Which of your two friends do you trust the most? Which of your two friends can offer you more protection? Which of your two friends has the most skills that you can use to survive? You need to be asking yourself these sorts of questions. You don't have the luxury of friends, Ellie. From now on its about survival!'

The old man quickly cast a glance up and down the shadowed walkway behind the stall. 'Once you're off this world Ellie, you have a chance of shaking them off. It's a big untamed universe out there. They will struggle to find you, but they'll keep looking for you, keep looking for you until they find you again.'

Mason's expression softened. 'I'm so sorry. They were never supposed to find out, not until it was too late. But they have, and that means you're in terrible danger, Ellie.'

He grabbed her shoulders firmly. 'Once you're out there, ' he said nodding upwards, 'stay away from the older, more stable worlds…seek chaotic places, worlds in turmoil, at war.'

'There aren't any wars,' said Ellie.

The old man shook his head. 'That's what they'd have you believe, Ellie, when you calmly sit at home and watch holovision - that everything is okay, at peace. But it's not. There are many worlds fighting brutally for their independence. And you must thank your lucky stars that, right now, that's the case....because in places like those you will have a chance to hide from *them*, you will find allies, people willing to help you stay hidden. Now please hurry up and...'

Ellie shook her head. 'Who are *they*? Please tell me.'

'Any world government, any authority, *the Administration*...it's all of them you need to watch out for Ellie. You must stay away from them until you are ready.'

'Ready for what?'

'Listen to the disc, later, when you've time. Listen to it carefully. Now, you must go back to your shuttle, bring with you the friend you can trust the most, and get to hangar 113 before the barge goes! Do you understand?'

'Are you coming?'

'No, I'll have to find my own way. It's you that's important right now. You, not me. Do you understand?'

Ellie nodded uncertainly, 'will I see you again?'

Mason shrugged, 'who knows?' He looked around anxiously. 'They're already here in Harvest City, you haven't much time. Now please, go!'

CHAPTER 20

Deacon stood over the control desk of the port guidance system and studied the various flickering displays. There were over a hundred of them.

'So think man, what vehicles have you seen come in this morning?' he asked with growing irritation.

The port controller looked up at him, his eyes shifting from one of the armed men to the next, clearly unsettled by the sight of them. 'M-many orbit-to-ground ones this morning. A l-lot of small travelling vehicles.'

'I'm after a white colored surface shuttle. Quite an old model.'

The controller nodded, eager to please, 'Yes…y-yes..I've had some sh-shuttles come in…v-various colors.'

Deacon attempted a disarming smile to encourage him. The fool was gibbering nervously like an idiot. The port controller was no use to him like that – too willing to say *yes* to any question asked. With hindsight, striding into the control room brandishing his credentials and flanked by armed mercenaries had probably been overkill. The port controller was trembling with fear, no doubt convinced that one of his little side-deals with black-market traders had been discovered.

'Look, all I'm interested in is a particular shuttle, ' said Deacon. The port controller seemed to relax a little on hearing that. 'Have you seen a *white* shuttle come in this morning? On the tail-plane and the wings it's marked *Goodman Tours*.'

The controller took a moment to consider the question. 'Uh...no, hang on! Yes, I th-think so. Yes, I think I-I saw a *white* one not long ago.'

Deacon placed a hand on the man's shoulder. 'Are you sure about that?'

He nodded.

Deacon smiled and patted him encouragingly. 'Good, very good. Now, if it wasn't too long ago, can you remember which hangar?'

The controller shook his head anxiously, bit his lip as he tried to recall.

'No, I thought not,' muttered Deacon. 'I presume you have monitoring equipment in every hangar?'

The controller smiled uncomfortably. 'In most of them, w-we do.'

Most of them. Yes, of course. It wouldn't be *all* of them. Deacon knew the way things worked on frontier worlds like these. There was always a little room for contraband to exist; a little margin for illegal trades, non-taxed goods. And that all happened in the few hangars where the monitoring equipment and surveillance cameras was supposedly 'awaiting routine maintenance'. The man fidgeting uncomfortably in front of him was no doubt skimming a little goodwill off of that.

'Well let's run through the monitors that *are* working first then. See if we can find that white shuttle still docked. Alright?'

The controller nodded.

'A white surface shuttle is what I'm after. See what you can find. Leonard?'

'Yes Deacon?'

'Give him a hand.'

The young lad settled in a seat beside the agitated controller and began to cycle through the monitored images of each occupied hangar. Deacon gazed at the flickering screens, as images of various vessels appeared one after the other on screen as they cycled through each surveillance channel

They're here somewhere. I know it.

They had come to Harvest City alright. Deacon had learned to trust his instincts; those, and Leonard's unique gift to crunch data and spot patterns in chaos, had so far steered them correctly, right across the galaxy to this planet.

And they'd landed bang on the money.

Yes, that bloody shuttle was here somewhere.

*

Ellie hurriedly pushed the trolley inside the hangar.

'What's the matter Ellie-girl?' called out Jez as she struggled after her with several swollen plastic shopping bags.

'The three of us have to talk, Jez, and *quickly*.'

She pushed the trolley across the floor of the hangar and, with a final burst of effort, up the ramp at the rear of the shuttle and into the passengers' suite. Jez labored inside after her and, with a gasp of relief, dropped the bags to the floor.

'What's the matter El'? You look like you've been mugged by a ghost.'

Ellie looked around. 'Where's Aaron?'

She hurried across the hold, opened the hatchway leading up into the cockpit and saw him checking the refueling status on a display panel. 'Aaron!' she called out, 'we need to talk!'

'Just a second,' he grunted back at her.

'No, it needs to be *now*!' she barked.

Aaron turned round with a concerned look on his face. Ellie realized she had all but screamed at him just then. The desperation in her voice was beginning to frighten her. He made his way back to the aft of the cockpit.

'What's the matter?' The expression of concern on his face suddenly intensified. 'Crap! Have you seen them? Are they here?'

Ellie shook her head. 'No, I dunno, maybe. But there is something else I need to talk to you about urgently. And Jez too.'

She beckoned Aaron into the hold. Jez and Aaron stared at her. 'What's happened?' asked Jez.

'That man who let us run for it, Jez? You know, back at the weather station...the mercenary?'

She nodded.

'There are others. Others trying to help me. There's a surface-to-orbit barge waiting for me in a hangar up at the other end of the port. It's waiting to take us up into orbit, to a freight ship. Someone has paid a lot of money for that, and it's only going to wait another,' Ellie checked the time, 'another half an hour.'

Aaron and Jez looked at each other.

'Ellie, this could be a trap,' Aaron said. 'Has someone just approached you?'

Jez looked sharply at him and then turned back to Ellie. 'Or it might *not* be a trap. You've got to go for it girl. That's your chance!'

'Ellie, you don't know where that barge will take you! Perhaps out into the middle of nowhere, and they'll finish you off there,' he said.

'Or, like that mercenary...this could be genuine; a chance for her to escape, Aaron. A chance to get away from whoever these...these people are!'

Ellie looked from one to the other. The decision, boiling away in her mind wasn't whether to go or not. That decision she had made within nanoseconds of turning away from the old man and heading for the hangar. No, the decision was *who* she was going to take with her.

'Ellie, this is not good. Who the hell did you speak to?' asked Aaron.

'A stranger, an old man. But I know his face from somewhere, I've met him before.'

'What? Where? Think Ellie...where?'

'I don't know. I can't remember!'

'She's got no choice Aaron. She *has* to trust him!' Jez turned to Ellie, and for the first time since they'd met, Ellie saw tears in her friend's eyes. 'Don't get me wrong, girl...I'm going to miss you an' everything,' Jez continued with a forced smile, 'but you're better off out there in the black than down stuck here.'

Aaron shook his head. 'The man could be one of *them*...you know? One of those men who were trying to gun you down back there? This is no time to be reckless. We can hide out somewhere remote and let this thing blow over!'

'We're utterly fregged if we stay here!' Jez shouted. 'How long do you think we'll last hiding out there in the fregging desert?! As soon as we come back to here for more supplies or New Haven, they'll have us!'

Ellie checked the time once more. It was running out for her.

*

'Hold it!' said Deacon. He walked across the floor to study the display in front of the controller. But by the time he got there, the man had cycled forward through another two or three hangars.

'Go back!'

The controller tapped an icon on screen and stepped back to the previous image, an empty hangar.

'Again.'

The image changed to show a shuttle, distinct with its pug nose and stubby delta wings. By the dim light in the hangar it didn't look as brilliantly white as it had out in the desert against the dark purple night sky. But that was definitely the one.

'Zoom in on that,' he said pointing to a company logo on one of the wings. The controller hit another icon on screen and the wing instantly magnified.

Goodman Tours.

'That's it,' he muttered, a smile spreading across his lean face. 'Which hangar is that sitting in?'

The controller checked another display. 'Hangar 47. That's down towards the far end of the concourse.'

Deacon studied the image for a few moments. He could see from the thick cord running across the hangar floor that the shuttle was refueling already. It wasn't here to stay then.

'Can you prevent it from taking off again?'

'Uh...n-no, not really,' the controller replied.

'Well, can we get some law marshals down there right now!?'

The controller looked up anxiously at Deacon. 'W-we could call the port m-marshal's station. But he's not often there.'

'You have just one marshal on duty here?!'

The man nodded uncomfortably, his face pinching into a wince.

Deacon ground his teeth with frustration. *This whole damned planet is a waste of bloody space.*

He stood up and turned round to face the mercenaries. 'Right, let's go. Hangar 47, now!'

He turned to Leonard. 'And Leonard you keep watching that image, let me know if anyone enters or leaves the hangar.'

'Yes Deacon.'

*

Twenty-five minutes left.

She had no idea how far up the concourse hangar 113 was, or how long it would take her to get there weaving her way through all those people. It was almost as crowded as the pedestrian ways back in New Haven.

Decision time Ellie.

That old man had advised her to pick someone she trusted, to pick someone who would best help her survive, who could do the most to protect her. He had advised her to be utterly selfish in deciding who of these two, her closest friends, should escape off-world with her. But there was more to the decision for Ellie, more to this than just her own survival. There was her family too. For the first time since scrambling for safety aboard the shuttle, it occurred to her that they might now be at risk too.

Why? Why? Why? What was so special about her? She could think of nothing she had done, or said, or seen or heard, nor anything she could possibly do in the future, that would make her so fregging important that someone would travel the universe to kill her; that *a whole planet* might be quarantined just to trap her? Was her family in danger too?

They must be.

She realized that whoever she left behind, Aaron or Jez, she would beg them to do their best to look after her family. The question she had to ask herself *now*...was which one of them could do the most to look after them; keep them safe?

'Jez, Aaron. The man said there's room for only two of us to go,' she said looking from one to the other, and realizing as she spoke, that she was already crying. 'I can only take *one* of you, and the other...I'm begging, please...will have to look after my family.'

Both Jez and Aaron started to reply but Ellie *shushed* them with a raised finger. 'I'm out of time!' she cried. 'I have to go now!'

They fell silent, as Ellie, still struggling inside with the decision, still not entirely sure which of them she needed by her side and which of them might best serve to protect her family...raised her finger. It wavered for a moment, almost as if it was doing the thinking for her.

Then her eyes locked on Aaron's. It could only be Aaron.

CHAPTER 21

Deacon led the armed men down through the crowded thoroughfare. At first, progress was painfully slow, requiring him more often than not to push the lumbering citizens out of his path. One burly looking shuttle pilot had barked out after him, telling Deacon he was going to teach him some manners. Deacon had dealt with him by giving a nod to one of his hired guns, who had casually pulled out his firearm and aimed it at the man. He disappeared into the crowd promptly.

He wasn't going to let her get away. Not again, not whilst he had breath and a pulse in his body. He ordered all his men to pull out their firearms so that everyone around could see them clearly. Deacon did likewise, pulling his sidearm out of his hip-holster, extracting an ammo cartridge from his waistcoat pocket and slamming it home. The loud click and hum of the weapon charging for use, and the sight of the three mercenaries brandishing their pulse rifles, effectively did the job. Now, as he called out sharply to people in front of them to move aside and make way for official port authority business, they did so quickly and quietly, eyeing the weapons warily.

As they broke into a jog, he looked up at the large hangar doors as they passed them, the odd numbers to the right, even to the left.

Ninety-five, ninety-four...

*

Aaron looked at her, struggling to keep a calm and casual smile on his rough and unshaven face. 'Of course I'll look after them, Ellie,' he replied. The terrible lie felt thick and oily on his tongue. When - if - she eventually found out that her family had all been slain, he knew she would never forgive him for keeping that news from her. He hated himself for lying to her like this.

'I'll make sure they're kept out of harm's way,' he mumbled, his eyes meeting Jez's for a moment.

'Thank you Aaron,' she said rushing forward and spreading her arms around his shoulders and holding onto him tightly. 'I owe you so much,' she whimpered into his chest.

'You just make sure you catch that barge, girl.'

'I will.'

He stroked her hair as she sobbed against him, dampening his oil-stained jump suit with tears. He looked up at Jez. 'You look after her for me.'

'Hey. You know I will,' said Jez with a hint of smile for him. 'You look after yourself too, big guy.'

He nodded and then pushed Ellie gently away. 'You'd better go now, Ellie.'

She nodded, 'I know.'

'And whatever this is all about, when it's done…and you're safe. Come back and see me, okay?'

'Okay.'

'We'll meet outside Dionysius. I'll buy the coffee.'

Ellie nodded, and a fresh tear rolled down her cheek. She laughed, 'not the cheap synthi-stuff next time. I can't stand it.'

'You got it,' he replied. 'Now go get your shoulder bag, and get out of here before you miss the barge.'

*

'Deacon? It's Leonard.'

He tapped the communicator on his wrist as he continued to jog down the concourse.

Eighty-one, eighty….

'Yes...what is it, Leonard?'

'There's something going on in the hangar, it looks like...yes, it looks like two people are coming out...two people leaving.'

'Leaving?'

'Yes, like some sort of a big goodbye. I saw some hugging and that. Two of them coming out of the hangar now.'

Deacon was breathing hard and was unbearably hot in his jacket and waistcoat. He was tempted to throw the jacket to the floor and retrieve it later, but it was worth far too much for that - real silk - he'd never see the thing again.

'What...do...they...look...like?' he gasped, each word punctuated by a labored breath.

'Hard to see, it's not a great angle. I think it's the two girls we tracked to that abandoned outpost.'

Ellie Quin and her friend once more. Where were they going? *They took a shuttle here, and now they were leaving that behind? Why?*

A cold stab of anxiety caused him to stop in his tracks. What if someone had a ship standing by? Whoever had organized that surface shuttle that had miraculously appeared in the middle of the desert, to whisk them to safety may also have organized surface-to-orbit transport.

Oh no, oh no. No.

The mercenaries had stopped with him and now turned, awaiting orders.

'You and you,' he said to two of them, 'stop that shuttle from leaving. Kill the pilot if necessary. Shoot the ship's engines out if necessary. Go!'

'Yes, sir.' The mercenaries turned round and hurried away with their weapons held out in front of them towards hangar 47.

Deacon turned to the third man - the mercenary he considered the most capable of the three, the most reliable; the one who had made a desperate last ditch attempt to prevent the girls getting away by scrambling onto the rising ramp of the shuttle as it lifted off.

'You're with me. We're looking for those two girls again. They're out here on this concourse, somewhere amongst these people. Keep your eyes open.'

'Yes, sir.'

*

They emerged from the hangar, each carrying only a single bag. Ellie took one last look back inside through the open door and waved at Aaron, wondering if she would ever see him again. Picking Jez to come with her had felt like the worst kind of betrayal, but only Aaron could go back to the farm and collect her family and take them somewhere safe, which he'd solemnly promised to do.

Oh crud, I'm so sorry, Aaron.

She waved once more, but this time instead of returning the wave, he gestured for her to get a move on.

Remember, time moves along quicker than you think, he had once told her. And that's what he was telling her again now.

'Come on, girl,' said Jez, grabbing her arm. 'We have to get a wiggle-on if we want to catch this barge of yours.'

Ellie checked the time again. There were twenty minutes to go until it was due to lift off, with or without them. 'Oh crud, we really have to hurry,' she said, 'it's up at the other end.'

They began to walk as swiftly as they could through the swirling mass of people. After a few moments pushing her way past several knots of people, Jez leant over and tapped Ellie's shoulder.

'Have you noticed?'

'What?'

'We look so-o-o-o-o New Haven.'

Ellie cast a glance down at her clothes and her bright green boots, and then at Jez, whose choice of garments was even louder. 'Oh, freg, you're right,' she replied. They stood out in the milling crowd around them like a glowing billboard.

'We need a little disguise.'

Ellie looked frantically around, aware that time was now working very much against them. She spotted a trading stall that sold the sort of clothing that Aaron and his fellow shuttle pilots seemed to like; tan colored flight jackets, olive colored boiler suits, dark plain caps, boots. Sensible, practical, durable…dull clothing.

'Wait a second,' she said to Jez before jogging across to the stall.

'Those jackets, how much?' she asked the trader, a short balding man with dark weathered skin.

'These? Six *dees* a piece, lady. You'll need an ultra-small though, let me look in the back I think I've got some that size.'

'No, it's alright, just give me two of those there,' she said pointing towards the closest jackets hanging on display.

'Uhh, way too big, honey, they're…'

'Just *do it!'* Ellie barked. The trader recoiled with surprise.

'I'm sorry,' Ellie continued, '…it's just….they're not for me, they're for my dad.'

'Ahhh, okay. Well, these are large, forty-two inch…'

'That's fine. Just his size, thanks.'

Ellie handed over a twenty Harper's Reach dee-note which the trader looked at uncertainly. 'You got anything smaller? I'm low on change right now.'

She bit her lip and smiled. 'Keep the change okay? I'm in a bit of a hurry.'

She returned to Jez moments later holding the jackets out in front of her.

'Oh you've got to be kidding?' said Jez grabbing hold of one of them and looking at the milling people around them. 'Ugghh, I'll look like one of these grubby mole-men.'

Ellie slid the over-large jacket on. It swamped her, covering her up almost down to her knees. Her green pvc boots still stood out conspicuously beneath her tan camouflage, but then she decided, within the press of people, few people were going to look down at her feet and see them. It would have to do for now anyway. Jez was almost as swamped by her jacket. She zipped up the front and pulled the hood up over her head.

'Let's go girl,' she said to Ellie, 'we've wasted too much time as it is.'

Ellie nodded, realizing how glad she was that Jez was coming with her; she couldn't do this all on her own.

They resumed making their way at a torturously slow speed up the concourse, passing hangar after hangar, Ellie counting them as they passed by.

Sixty-two, sixty-three.

CHAPTER 22

Aaron watched her disappear from view. He knew instinctively that this was the last time he would see either of the girls. They couldn't come back to Harpers Reach, not ever, and Aaron couldn't see a way to get off-world. He watched the movement of people outside through the open door of the hangar, half hoping Ellie would return, half hoping she didn't. Jez was right. His hiding-out-in-the-wilderness plan was mere desperation. The law marshals would catch up with them eventually. Ellie needed to get off-world as quickly as possible. If those people out there after her were really working for the authorities....*the Administration*, then it probably wouldn't take them long to zero in on them again down here on this empty planet. There really wasn't anywhere to hide down here.

And then what?

That was obvious, the same fate that Ellie's family had met. These people weren't leaving any talking mouths in their wake. He realized he was as much a target now without Ellie, as he had been with her.

Aaron walked across the hangar floor and disconnected the fuel hose from the belly of his shuttle. He dragged it back across the hangar floor, out of the way. He deliberately made the transaction electronically for the fuel and the stopover fee, perhaps that would draw Ellie's pursuers his way and buy the girls a little more time.

He was good to go now.

But where?

Now there's a question. The choices weren't exactly great. The best thing to do right now, would be to find somewhere remote, quiet and think it out. Actually, maybe the first thing he'd do is head over to Ellie's old home, the farm, and bury those people he had heard so much about, but never met. It didn't seem right that the farm would be left like that, with the enviro-dome door sitting open and valuable air leaking out….those people left on the ground where they had fallen. Aaron felt the need to tidy things up there for perpetuity. Maybe one day, if he met Ellie again, at least he'd be able to say to her that he took care of things, saw to her folks, turned everything off sealed-up the farm for good.

He climbed up the ramp, through the passengers' suite, looking briefly around the clean, white and comfortable interior.

The snow-tours thing didn't last very long did it?

He shook his head sadly, they could have made a small fortune doing that for a few years, maybe even enough to expand the business, buy another shuttle.

Oh well.

He climbed through the bulkhead into the cockpit, sat down in his seat and prepared to go quickly through the brief pre-launch checks.

*

Deacon cast a quick glance across the way at the mercenary stationed opposite.

A good man.

All three of them had been recruited from a pool based on Liberty. They were all security-approved, they had all been used previously for dirty work, each with a track record of efficiently performed assassinations. They were all ex-marines, fit and well trained but, of the three, this one across the way seemed to be the sharpest of the bunch. He was scanning the crowd with a systematic sweep, first one way, slowly, then back again, like a sniper looking for a valid target. Deacon had read the dossiers on all three of the mercenaries he had been sent. And this one, Asset #2, had served several years in some of the Administration's most elite military units.

Deacon felt confident that the job of combing the passing crowd for those two girls was being done efficiently from his side of the concourse.

Deacon and the mercenary were stationed outside hangars ninety-six and seven; a point where this wide concourse narrowed somewhat, pushing the passing shoppers, travelers, tradesmen, pilots, crews and passengers into a compact river of ambling, unhurried movement. But it still wasn't going to be easy spotting them. He had a holographic image of Ellie Quin, a forty-five degree rotation from the front round to one side, taken when she had first entered New Haven nine months ago. The hair had been shorter then from what he had managed to see of her at a distance as she scrambled aboard the shuttle. Her friend, as yet - no name identified, a striking-looking young woman, a foot taller, close on six feet, again with fashionably cut hair a little longer than Quin's. But it was their clothes from New

Haven that would scream out amongst the crowd. Unless there had been a change of clothes aboard the shuttle in which they had escaped, the taller girl had been wearing a neon yellow plastic top with a distinctive 'y' strap up the back, the last time he had seen her. That's what he needed to look for then, a splash of that unique, eye-searing neon yellow.

Silly girls.

They would have to squeeze through this narrow choke-point if they were going anywhere. He shot a glance at the mercenary leaning discreetly against the wall on the other side of the thoroughfare, scanning the passing foot trade intensely.

I've got a good man there.

Between them, there was no way past for the girls. This was where he'd reacquire her again. It was probably going to be a bloody, messy and very public execution. A discreet finish to the job would have satisfied his professional pride. But given how things might have gone, if this girl had managed to find a way off-world…

The thought made the hairs on his forearms rise.

*

Deacon had to concede he had been lucky. Arriving here an hour later he would have missed her. She'd be somewhere in orbit, and probably gone from this system before the blockade could be out in place. With hindsight, he shouldn't have been worrying about taking a low-profile approach. This planet was nothing. Garbage. Old Earth language had a curious but apt-sounding aphorism for this sort: *trailer trash*.

What he *should* have done from the start was to have arrived on this planet with an entire marine group, instantly locked down the world with a quarantine order and then, with ground troops, grid-searched New Haven from top to bottom, then Harvest City.

He had been *very* lucky not to lose her.

*

Ninety-two and ninety-three...
They were making painfully slow progress squeezing their way up towards the other end of the port. Ellie checked the time once more. They had seven minutes left.

'Oh crud, Jez, we're going to *miss it*!' she said under her breath. 'We need to go faster!'

Ellie stood on tiptoes to look ahead. 'Oh great, there's a bottle-neck up in front of us.'

'Well, why don't we go round the back of the market stalls instead?' asked Jez.

As Ellie had done earlier - only to bump into that strange old man in the dark, litter-strewn gap between the back of the stall and the large grimy wall of the concourse. She wondered who else they might bump into doing that again. But with only seven minutes left, there was no choice.

'Okay,' she said, pushing her way through the pedestrians, out of the flow and towards the wall to their left. They pushed through the gap between two stalls, and then Ellie cautiously poked her head around the back, looking left and right. A few other people were walking up and down this narrow, dim, passageway, equally frustrated by the crush of people out front. She saw a few traders pulling stock out of crates stacked behind their stalls. But it was empty enough that they could make faster time jogging along it.

'We should run,' said Ellie.

Jez pushed past her. 'Okay, but let me go first, I'll scare anyone out of our way,' said Jez breaking into a jog, her platform boots *clacking* loudly off the metal floor.

Ellie followed in her wake, offering an apologetic smile to those few people they passed by, pressed awkwardly up against the wall to let them through.

'They're much more polite here than in New Haven,' Jez shouted back over her shoulder.

Ninety-four, ninety-five...

They passed behind a stall selling music chips. Most of it was pirated and imported from other worlds by the look of the crates of goods out the back of the stall. She heard the muted twittering sounds of the Crazie-Beanie song blasting out from speakers around the front of the stall, and realized, finally, she'd heard the damned tune enough.

CHAPTER 23

Aaron noticed the handshake icon on screen, and a moment later, he felt the thrusters surge to life as the automated port guidance system assumed control of his shuttle. Lisa rose slowly off the pad amidst a cloud of steam and dust.

The shuttle's pug nose tilted forward slightly as the guidance system slowly turned his craft around to head out of the opening hangar doors.

Aaron watched out of the window as the orange glare of the world outside the hangar slid into view. The hangar doors finished opening, and almost immediately, he felt the gentle push of the aft thrusters easing the shuttle out into the late afternoon sunlight. He felt the warmth on his face and hands as the cockpit filled with light.

Something glinted beside him, and he looked across to his right at the co-pilot's seat. On the ripped and threadbare seat, beside the spring that stood out through the upholstery, he noticed a small piece of plastic jewelry. It was one of those thin, stretchy Beanie-bangles that Ellie liked wasting her money on. He reached across and picked it up, turning it over in his hand to look at the silly character-logo on the thickest part of the round gel strip.

He smiled and shook his head. Ellie loved that stupid damned character; a pointless irritating mascot created to help sell a cleaning product, and now it seemed stuck on the side of everything. For some reason, he felt compelled to hang on to it. He slid it over his left hand, the stretchy plastic struggling to accommodate his wide knuckles, then it slid easily past the rest of his hand and settled around his wrist.

His control panel chimed and the handshake icon was replaced with the release icon, Lisa was once more in his control. Staring out at the empty world ahead of him, he set off, knowing where he wanted to go first. There was a family out there that deserved a decent burial. He took the control yoke and headed west, hugging the arid ground.

*

'Deacon?'

He touched his earpiece. 'Yes, what is it *now* Leonard?'

'The shuttle left before our men could stop it.'

Dammit.

'Did anyone get back on it?' he asked.

'Not that I could see. Just the pilot.'

That was another loose end he was going to have to track down and sort out, but not now. Ellie Quin was still here, and she was the principal target. The shuttle pilot could be picked up later. Harpers Reach was a poor place to try and hide.

'Thanks Leonard,' he replied.

He concentrated once more on the narrow choke-point in front of him. The faces streaming past were more frequently male than female, varying skin hues. There were almost as many off-world types here as in the other city. Every now and then, Deacon's eyes would pick out a feminine face, and for a moment, he felt a prickling spark of exhilaration until further examination revealed the face was not one of the two he was after.

Keep looking for that neon yellow, he reminded himself. A feminine face, and a splash of that distinctive bright yellow amidst that crowd, and he'd have them.

Music from a stall a little further down had started playing - a twittering, gibbering hi-pitched voice on top of a deep pounding bass line, that he could feel as much as hear. It was already giving him a headache. Worse still, he suspected the mind-numbing melody, if it could be called that, lurking in that cacophony somewhere would undoubtedly plague him all the way back home to Liberty, until he could settle back in his comfortable apartment once more and dislodge it with the sophisticated melodies and rhythms of a little late twentieth century Drum-n-Bass.

Do people really call this twittering moronic crap...music?

He heard something else though, faintly at first, ebbing and flowing behind the noise of the market place and that damned jingle. Something new....*clatter-clack, clatter-clack, clatter-clack;* the sound of heeled shoes on metal, someone running...someone in a hurry. It drew his attention and he leant forward and looked down in the direction from which the faint noise was approaching, looking for the bobbing head of someone on the run, but saw nothing.

*

Jez drew up short and Ellie piled into the back of her.

'What are you stopping for, Jez?' she yelled. Jez was silent, frozen in place.

'Jez? What is it?' Ellie stepped around her friend and saw *him* standing a dozen paces in front of them, his gun held out ready, his eyes locked on theirs.

'It's *him*,' hissed Jez, 'one of the men from the weather station.'

Ellie recognized him, even though she had only seen his face for a few moments by a torchlight that had jumped and danced erratically in the dark. It was the man who had let them go. He kept his eyes on them, with no flicker of reaction on his features.

Ellie hesitantly pointed up towards the top end of the concourse, the gesture was a question.

Will you let us go again?

She put her hands together as if praying.

Please.

There was no reaction from the man for several long seconds. And then with the slightest nod, and the lowering of his weapon by a few degrees, he wordlessly assented, the gesture almost imperceptible.

They moved warily towards him, squeezing past, their eyes locked alternately on his eyes and the gun he continued to hold ready. Jez winked at him and blew him a kiss and Ellie mouthed *thank you* and then they were on their way again, glancing backwards once more to be sure he hadn't suddenly changed his mind and was lining up a shot on them. They broke into a run once more

*

Clatter-clack, clatter-clack, clatter-clack

The noise was coming from the other direction now. He turned to look *up* the concourse and for a fleeting moment, between two stalls on the far side of the choke-point he saw the bobbing heads of two girls, and the tiniest flash of neon yellow as a drab-colored jacket flapped to one side.

It's them! How did they get past us? Shit!

He pulled his weapon out and fired a burst up into the air.

The effect was instantaneous. As the deafening and distinctive rattle of several gunshots echoed off the walls, the entire river of people in front of him dropped to the ground, a hundred feet in either direction. Further away, people froze and looked round to see what the noise was.

Only two people within sight were still on the move, now running as fast as they could.

'Over there!' he shouted to his man across the way, and pointed towards the two girls. 'AFTER THEM!'

Deacon broke into a run on his side of the thoroughfare, not wanting to be slowed down by having to wade across a mass of prone people to join his man. The mercenary began to run after them, faltering here and there as he wound his way past cowering stall holders and stacks of goods.

Deacon looked ahead. He could hear the noise of those hard-heeled boots clattering and scraping ahead, amidst the tremulous hush that had descended on the formerly busy thoroughfare. He caught another glimpse of their bobbing heads up in front as they passed between two stalls. He was gaining on them, a little.

God these girls can run.

In a heartbeat he decided they were close enough to take a shot. Sliding to a halt, he braced his weapon hand against the post of a market stand and lined up along the short barrel of his gun at a larger gap between two stalls on the far side, *ahead* of where he had last seen them, and waited, holding his breath to steady his aim. Waiting for them to step into his aim.

Oh-crud-oh-crud-oh-crud!

Ellie staggered behind Jez, already winded. Jez was making better speed than she was. But every now and then she slowed and turned round to check Ellie was right behind her. 'Keep running girl!' she yelled.

They heard the rattle of a pulse rifle behind them, and the wall several feet above them sparked with the impact of a dozen poorly aimed shots.

Ellie shot a glance over her shoulder. The man who had let them past was now after them, but making slower progress than she would have thought.

Deliberately slow?

'Don't worry Ellie, I think he's aiming high,' shouted Jez back at her. 'Just keep going, we're nearly there!'

Ellie looked up at the hanger door they were racing by.

One hundred and five. She hoped that the barge was actually ready to go. It had better be or they were both going to be screwed.

What if there is no barge? She banished the thought from her mind. They had made their play, rolled the dice and that was all there was to it. She suddenly recalled that bizarre fortune-telling session Jez had dragged her along to. The boojam fortune teller had said she would make it into space, and if you believed that kind of hooey it looked like he'd got it right. But she wondered why the hell it hadn't occurred to him to warn her that it might be a somewhat hasty departure.

Jez turned round, grinning like a fool. That was Jez all over – her stress response was to leer like an idiot.

'Hey limp-chik, bet you didn't think we'd be doing this...'

The metal wall to her left exploded in a shower of sparks as a rapid-fired volley of high caliber projectiles slammed in from somewhere on the far side of the concourse. Jez flew back against the wall as if some giant invisible mallet had swung down and caught her in the midriff. She slid down onto her bottom, clutching her side and looking down angrily at the blood spilling into her cupped hands.

'Ouch!' she said spitting out flecks of crimson onto her pale chin.

Ellie knelt down beside her. 'Oh Jez, please...no!'

She looked up at Ellie panting wildly, and then nodded towards the way ahead. Ellie could see it now, could see what Jez was pointing out...the door to hangar 113, only fifty yards away. *Just there*. She turned back to look down at Jez, knowing in her heart what her friend was urging her to do.

'I'm can't leave you Jez, I'm not going to leave-'

'I'm not asking you to fregging leave me here! I want you to get me up dammit!' she spat the words out accompanied by a globule of blood. Ellie pulled Jez to her feet, and she shrieked with the pain. 'Go...go go!!!'

They staggered towards the doorway, as another volley of fire peppered the wall and the ground, and showers of sparks danced around them.

*

The mercenary watched the painfully slow progress the two girls were making up ahead of him. He had no idea where exactly it was they were making for. If it was the entrance to the city, then they had no hope at all. That was right up at the far end, another four or five hundred yards....might as well be a hundred miles away as far as things looked for them now.

Shit.

These girls weren't going to get away, not like this. It was all over for them. *Nice try, ladies*, but it wasn't going to happen; which was bad news all around. His really big pay check, the one that dwarfed the generous payment he was getting from the Administration for assisting the guy in the smart dark suit track down and kill this girl, was based on *the target* getting off-world alive. All bets on that big payday were history now. He had already pushed his luck as far as it should go letting them come past him. The guy in the smart dark suit must now be wondering whose side he was playing for. Very dangerous. He'd have a suspicion. There was nothing for it now. He needed to be the one to finish them off, to dispel any suspicions the man might have of him.

Time to cut your losses, and bring them down.

He knelt down and pulled his rifle up to aim at the backs of both of the girls, a pathetically easy shot to take. This wasn't going to be a kill he was ever going to be particularly proud of.

And then without warning they slid sideways out of view.

*

Ellie looked up at the barge ahead of them inside hangar 113. 'We're here Jez! There it is!'

Jez looked up at it. The engines were already rising in pitch, the loading ramp was still down, but warning lights were flashing above the cargo hold entrance. It was an automated barge, no crew, no pilot, no one to plead with to give them just another few seconds to make it across the landing pad. It was going to leave at exactly the scheduled time, not a second earlier, nor a second later. Launch time was merely seconds away.

They had to run for it now.

'Come on Jez! We need to hurry!' Ellie manhandled her friend across the floor of the hangar towards the barge, as a shrill warning beacon began to sound inside the large hangar.

'Oh no! Don't leave!!!!' Ellie cried out as she struggled with legs that felt like lead and grunted with the exertion of carrying the dead weight of Jez.

The timbre of the engines increased in pitch and volume and the shrill wail of the warning siren was all but drowned out. With a loud clank and a whine of motors, the loading ramp began to rise.

Ellie hurled herself and Jez forward and, with a sense of *déja vu*, they collapsed onto the corrugated surface of the ramp and, as it swung swiftly upwards, were unceremoniously rolled down into the cargo hold inside. With a loud clang the ramp locked home, and locking clamps outside slid shut.

*

Deacon staggered into the hangar, breathless from the final frantic sprint up the way, and having had to manhandle his way through the crowd. The mercenary was there already, standing just inside the doorway. Deacon noticed a dozen bullet casings scattered around the man's feet.

'Did you get them?' he shouted into the mercenary's ear, competing with the roar of engines of the barge as it lifted off the pad, tilted forwards and glided out through the opening doors of the hangar.

The mercenary hesitated almost imperceptibly. 'Yeah, I think I might have winged the smaller one, just as the barge's loading ramp closed.'

They both looked up at the dwindling barge, rising rapidly into the peach sky, leaving a contrail in its wake, as the doors of the hangar began to close once more.

'You *winged* her? Do you think it was a fatal shot?' he asked as he fought a little more air into his beleaguered lungs.

'Hard to say, sir.'

The hangar bay doors closed again swiftly with a loud reverberating rattle, shutting off their view of the barge, now little more than a black dot in the sky. Deacon sighed and shook his head. Mason's little creation had managed to bolt for it after all.

This was one of the contraband hangars, of that he was almost certain. So, that meant there was going to be no record of the ship in orbit that this barge belonged to, nor any details of its flight plans.

'Fine…if that's how we're going to play it,' he muttered to himself. 'Fine.' He suddenly found himself laughing…a desperate wheeze of a laugh; a spasm of exhaustion, released tension and a hint of exasperation, or maybe all three.

'If that's how you want to play it…I'll just have to quarantine every other fucking planet in this damned system.'

He could do it. He had the goddamned authority to do it.

CHAPTER 24

Ellie stared out of the tiny, grime-encrusted porthole at the receding world outside. Here it was, the moment she had been fantasizing about for as long as she could remember, the moment she finally waved goodbye to Harpers Reach. In her fantasies, the window through which she would see it all gradually dwindle away to nothing more than a dusty red spot in space, had been big; a large viewing bay in some luxurious inter-system pleasure cruiser, surrounded by the great and the beautiful. And in this particular escape-from-this-cruddy-world fantasy, that she had played over and over in her head countless times since she was old enough to realize there was a much larger world beyond her immediate horizon, she had not been cradling the blood-spattered face of her closest, her *only* friend.

'Can you see it Jez? We finally made it off-world, just as we said we would,' she said gently stroking her pale cheek. 'We did it!'

Jez groaned fitfully and opened her eyes to stare out at the sight. She smiled up at Ellie and nodded. 'Yeah, we did it girl. Not just cube-chiks now....we're space-chiks,' she replied weakly. A droplet of blood trickled from her nose, and rolled down across her face into Ellie's lap. It left a trail almost as dark as Jez's favorite shade of lipstick.

'Shhhhh. Rest now Jez....You'll be alright. I know you will. We'll get you a doctor or med-unit onboard the ship. You're going to be fine.'

Jez nodded, closed her eyes, and settled gently in Ellie's lap, her breathing growing quieter, fainter.

Ellie fumbled in her pocket for the data-disc the old man had handed her. She pulled it out and slotted into her palm-dictionary. One file. An audio file...

'For twenty years I've been agonizing over how exactly I was going to tell you about who you are...what you are. For twenty years, I've only ever known you as L-239-HR-2457709....and since I've been here observing you, I've learned that your parents called you Ellie.'

'So, now I have a name...Ellie, perhaps it's time now that I introduce myself and tell you a little about who you are.

My name is Edward Mason. You came to me as a paternity request and I personally processed you. Before you ask...yes...you are a product of your parent's genes. You ARE their child. But you're also a bit more.

You're special Ellie, so very special. You are the only way humanity is going to survive.

So you have to stay alive.

'You have to travel Ellie. You have to run. And you'll have to be so very careful. The Administration, know everything about you and they'll do anything to find you, and to kill you.'

'I had hoped that you would never need know of these things, or even to know of me...I had planned always to watch you from afar, help you discreetly....ensuring the winding path you travelled through Human Space was trouble free. But that's all changed now that they know. I'm so sorry. Now you'll have to scamper and hide from the Administration's bloodhounds, like some kind of vermin. And they'll never give up on you. But Ellie...you must travel, you must. The only advice I can give you is to seek the worlds in our universe that are torn and troubled...and my god Ellie, there are so many out there - Human Space is falling apart. But you wouldn't believe that from what you see on the toob, eh?'

'Fly Ellie, fly away as fast and as far as you can. And stay alive as long as you can. God, I wish there was more I could do to help you.'

No more. That was all there was. That seemed to be it.

Her thumb absently thumbed the record switch of her diary as she looked down at Jez. 'So, I'm...I'm someone's weapon? Is that it?' she laughed bitterly. 'Hufty, it's me. I just found out I'm some sort of virus, or something. That's what I am. A fregging weapon someone's made. Boring old Ellie Quin.'

Her gaze settled on Jez. 'Hey Jez, did you hear any of that stuff on the disc?'

Jez was still.

'Jez?'

She was perfectly still now.

'Oh God...Oh crud. Hufty, I think she's...she'd dead! Her blood's all over my lap. It's all over me. Oh no...please don't leave me alone in here, please don't die!'

She patted Jez's cheek. 'Jez? Wake up! Can you hear me? Please...oh crud! Please don't die!'

Nothing. She clamped her hands to her face. 'I really can't do this on my own. Not without you. I'm just nothing. I'm stupid and lost…and I want to go back home! Please…don't die, don't leave me alone here. Ple-e-e-ease!!!!'

Her voice sounded shrill. Echoing back at her from the hard metal bulkheads.

It's over, limp-chik. This is how it ends. Now just calm down and let it happen the way it's supposed to happen. You can't fight fate, Ellie girl. You can't fight fate.

It was dad's voice. Soothing, reassuring.

'I suppose you can't,' she whispered to herself. She thumbed the palm-diary off and put it in her pocket. Just her and Jez now. Just them. She stroked Jez's dark hair absently, all of a sudden resigned and quite ready to face to whatever future was ahead of her.

'We did it in the end, though, Jez, didn't we? You and me? We managed to get offworld.'

A solitary tear rolled down her cheek, past lips pressed grimly together, onto her small pointed chin, dimpled and creased as she struggled to hold herself together. It clung to her for a moment before splashing down on to Jez.

With a soft groan Jez stirred painfully. 'Ughhh…this would be such a great moment to savor, if this didn't hurt so fregging much, and you weren't dribbling on my face.'

OMNIPEDIA:
[Human Universe: digital encyclopedia]

Article: 'The Legend of Ellie Quin'

The trail of Ellie Quin grows warm again after she leaves the frontier world of Harpers Reach. It is perhaps a great tragedy that few records or data from that world survive to this day, that we may pore through and try to construct a more complete picture of what her life was like as a child on the colonial farm, and more importantly, what she did, what she saw, heard, smelled, experienced in that long dead city.

But that world belonged to Ellie Quin's childhood and, once she finally passed through the weak embrace of its atmosphere, it would never again feature in her short yet fantastic life.

Ahead of her lay a destiny of far greater magnitude and affect, than perhaps any other human in history could lay claim to.

Many scholars have argued that the time she spent there in New Haven forged the personality that would later have such an utterly complete impact on Human History.

Of course others have argued that everything that made Ellie Quin into Ellie Quin was already inside her from birth; perhaps the best example of the age-old nature versus nurture debate.

There are a few biographers, however, who suggest that most of the qualities that made her such an inspirational historical character lay inside her, inert, waiting to be awoken. But it was the experiences that lay in her immediate *future* as she headed away from Harpers Reach that would awaken within her the things that would eventually make her great, and change things so completely, that we, many centuries later still owe her memory our undying gratitude.

To be continued…..

In

ELLIE QUIN: BEYOND THE GATEWAY
(Book 4 of the Ellie Quin Series – coming SOON!)

ELLIE QUIN: BEYOND THE GATEWAY
(Book 4 in the Ellie Quin series – coming SOON)

Ellie and Jez have managed to escape the planet of Harpers Reach and find themselves on 'GateWay' – a floating megacity in space. Home of this solar system's media companies and digi-stream broadcasters.

Jez is talent-spotted by a producer who promises to make her a superstar. Meanwhile Ellie is discovering Human Space is nothing like how the newsies and sopa-drams depict it.

And Deacon, having lost Ellie's scent finally picks up on it again.

There's only one way out of this system for the girls…but will they find it in time?

Coming soon!

ALSO BY ALEX SCARROW

THREE TEENAGERS HAVE CHEATED DEATH.

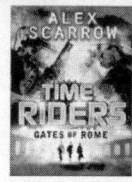

NOW THEY MUST STOP TIME TRAVEL DESTROYING THE WORLD.

BECOME A TIMERIDER @
www.time-riders.co.uk
Your first mission awaits . . .

Time travel is already happening, there are already people coming through from our future into our past...and they are corrupting it, contaminating it. But, a small covert agency has been set up to preserve our history and our timeline: the TimeRiders.

Embark on a profoundly exciting journey through history with this nine book series published by Puffin. Available on Amazon Kindle, iBookstore, and in print in all good book stores.

4239970R00138

Printed in Great Britain
by Amazon.co.uk, Ltd.,
Marston Gate.